Dear Reader,

This is my 90th book, so I wanted it to be special—a little bit different. I've never shied away from tricky issues, and I love to read stories about relationships that have been dragged back from the brink, but this one proved challenging to write for many reasons.

It's so easy to take each other for granted, just to assume you're all going in the same direction, but what if you're not? And what if, just when you tackle that issue, something far, far bigger intrudes and puts everything into perspective?

This is the story of Andy and Lucy Gallagher: a couple with three children, a marriage in meltdown and a potentially life-changing disease that strikes when they're at their lowest ebb. Andy survives, but will he ever be the same? And can their love cope with the changes that follow?

I hope you find their journey as thought-provoking, moving and emotional to read about as I found it to write, and that you come out at the end believing, as I do, that love can conquer everything life throws at it if you want it to. And that, for me, is the key to the universe.

Love

Caroline

FROM CHRISTMAS TO ETERNITY

BY
CAROLINE ANDERSON

First published in Great Britain 2012
by Mills & Boon, an imprint of Harlequin (UK) Limited.
Harlequin (UK) Limited, Eton House, 18-24 Paradise Road,
Richmond, Surrey TW9 1SR

© Caroline Anderson 2012

ISBN: 978 0 263 22899 1

Harlequin (UK) policy is to use papers that are natural, renewable and recyclable products and made from wood grown in sustainable forests. The logging and manufacturing process conform to the environmental regulations of the country of origin.

Printed and bound in Great Britain
by CPI Antony Rowe, Chippenham, Wiltshire

Caroline Anderson has the mind of a butterfly. She's been a nurse, a secretary, a teacher, run her own soft furnishing business, and now she's settled on writing. She says, 'I was looking for that elusive something. I finally realised it was variety, and now I have it in abundance. Every book brings new horizons and new friends, and in between books I have learned to be a juggler. My teacher husband John and I have two beautiful and talented daughters, Sarah and Hannah, umpteen pets, and several acres of Suffolk that nature tries to reclaim every time we turn our backs!' Caroline also writes for the Mills & Boon® Cherish™ series.

This is Caroline's 90th book for Mills & Boon!

Recent titles by Caroline Anderson:

Mills & Boon® Medical Romance™

THE FIANCÉE HE CAN'T FORGET
TEMPTED BY DR DAISY
ST PIRAN'S: THE WEDDING OF THE YEAR
THE SURGEON'S MIRACLE

Mills & Boon® Cherish™

THE VALTIERI BABY
VALTIERI'S BRIDE
THE BABY SWAP MIRACLE
MOTHER OF THE BRIDE

**These books are also available in eBook format
from www.millsandboon.co.uk**

Grateful thanks to Dr Jonathan Messenger
for his help with the neurological issues,
to James Woledge for pointing me in his direction,
and to my editor, Sheila Hodgson, who over the years
has tolerated with good grace
my terminal inability to deliver on time.

Thank you, all.

CHAPTER ONE

'Hi, this is the Gallaghers' phone, leave a message and we'll get back to you.'

Andy glanced at the clock and frowned. Six o'clock? When did that happen? And of course she wasn't answering, she'd be feeding and bathing the children. Just as well, perhaps. He knew she'd go off the deep end but there was nothing he could do about it. No doubt she'd add it to the ever-growing list of his failings, he thought tiredly, and scrubbed a hand through his hair.

'Luce, don't bother to cook for me, the locum's bailed so I'm covering the late shift. I'll grab something here and I'll see you at midnight.'

He slid the phone back into his pocket and shut his eyes for a moment.

He didn't need this. He had an assignment to finish writing by tomorrow for a course he'd stupidly undertaken, but they were a doctor down and it was Friday night. And Friday night in A&E was best friends with hell on earth, so there was no way he could leave it to a junior doctor.

For the hundredth time he wished he hadn't taken on the course. Why had he thought it was a good idea? Goodness knows, except it would give him another skill that would benefit his patients—assuming he was still alive by the end of it and Lucy hadn't killed him.

He heard the doors swish open, and knew it was kicking off already.

'Right, what have we got?' he asked, turning towards the trolley that was being wheeled in.

'Twenty-year-old male driver of a stolen car versus brick wall.' The paramedic rattled off the stats while Andy did a quick visual check.

Not good. Hoping it wasn't an omen for the coming night, he gave a short sigh and started work. Again.

'Noooooooo! Oh, Andy, no, you can't do this to me!' Lucy wailed, and sat down with a plop on the bottom step.

A little bottom wriggled onto the step beside her, Emily's hip nudging hers as she cuddled in close. 'What's wrong, Mummy? Has Daddy been naughty?'

She gritted her teeth. Only her staunch belief in presenting a united front stopped her from throwing him to the wolves, but she was so tempted. He absolutely deserved it this time.

'Not naughty, exactly. He's forgotten he's babysitting you while I go out, and he's working another shift.'

'Well, he can't,' Em said with the straightforward logic of the very young. 'Not if he promised. That's what he tells us. "You can't break a promise." So he has to do it. Ring him and tell him.'

If only it were that easy. She stared at Em, her hair scraped into messy bunches that sprouted from her head at different heights. She'd tied them in ribbons and Lucy knew it would take an age to get the knots out, but she didn't care. Just looking at her little daughter made her heart squeeze with love.

'Go on, Mummy. Ring him.'

Could it be that straightforward?

Maybe.

She called him back, and it went straight to voicemail. No surprises there, then. She sucked in a breath and left a blunt message.

'Andy, you promised to babysit tonight. I've got book club at seven thirty. You'll have to get someone else to cover.'

She hung up, and smiled down at Emily. 'There.'

'See?' Em said, grinning back. 'Now he'll *have* to come home.'

Lucy had her doubts. Where work was concerned, everything—everybody—else came second. She fed the children, ran the bath and dunked Lottie in it, then left the girls playing in the water while she gave the baby her night-time feed, and still he hadn't called.

She wasn't surprised. Not by that. What surprised her was that even now he still had the power to disappoint her...

It took an hour to assess and stabilise the driver, and just five seconds to check his phone and realise he was in nearly as much trouble as the young man was.

He phoned Lucy again, and she answered on the first ring.

'Luce, I'm sorry—'

'Never mind being sorry. Just get home quickly.'

'I can't. I told you. I'm needed to cover the department.'

'No. *Somebody's* needed to cover the department. It doesn't have to be you.'

'It does if I'm the only senior person available. Just get another babysitter. It can't be that hard.'

'At this short notice? You're kidding. Why can't you get another doctor? It can't be that hard,' she parroted back at him.

He sighed and rammed his hand through his hair again, ready to tear it out. 'I think a babysitter might be a little easier to find than an ED consultant,' he said crisply, nodding at the SHO who was waving frantically at him. 'Sorry, got to go. I'll see you later.'

Lucy put the phone down and looked into her baby's startlingly blue eyes. 'Oh, Lottie, what are we going to do with him?' she asked with a slightly shaky sigh.

The baby giggled and reached up a chubby fist to grab her hair.

'Don't you laugh at me,' she said, prising the sticky little fingers off and smiling despite herself. 'You're supposed to be asleep, young lady, and your daddy's supposed to be at home and I'm supposed to be going out to my book club. But that doesn't matter, does it? It doesn't matter what I want to do, because I'm at the bottom of the heap, somewhere underneath Stanley.'

The young black Lab, sitting by her leg doing a passable imitation of a starving rescue case, wagged his tail hopefully when he heard his name.

No wonder! Guilt washed over her, and she swallowed down the suddenly threatening tears.

'Sorry, boy,' she crooned, scratching his ears. 'I'm a rotten mum. Five minutes, I promise.'

She settled the yawning baby in her cot, fed the poor forgotten dog and then headed upstairs again to herd Emily and Megan out of the bath and into bed. She'd try ringing round a few friends. There must be *someone* who wasn't doing anything this evening who owed her a favour.

Apparently not.

So she phoned and apologised to Judith, and then changed into her pyjamas and settled down in front of the television with a glass of wine, a bar of chocolate and a book.

She might not be going out tonight, but she was blowed if she was working. Stuff the ironing. Stuff the washing up. Stuff all of it. As far as she was concerned, she was out, and it would all still be there in the morning.

Angry, defiant and underneath it all feeling a little sad for everything they'd lost, she rested her head back against the snuggly chenille sofa cushion and let out a long, unsteady sigh.

They'd had a good marriage once; a really good marriage.

It seemed like a lifetime ago...

The house was in darkness.

Well, of course it was. Even if she'd managed to get a babysitter, she'd have been back long ago. He pressed the remote control and the garage door slid open and slid shut again behind him as he switched off the engine and let himself into the house through the connecting door.

There was a bottle of wine on the side, a third of it gone, and the remains of a chocolate wrapper. The kitchen was a mess, the dishwasher hanging open, half loaded, the plates licked clean by Stanley.

The dog ambled out of his bed and came wagging up, smiling his ridiculous smile of greeting, and Andy bent down and rubbed his head.

'Hello, old son. Am I sleeping with you tonight?' he asked softly, and Stanley thumped his tail against the cupboard doors, as if the idea was a good one.

Not for the future of their marriage, Andy thought with a sigh, and eyed the bottle of wine.

It was after midnight. Quite a lot after. And he still had to finish the assignment. God, he was tired. Too tired to do it, too wired to sleep.

He took a glass out of the cupboard, sloshed some wine into it and headed for the study. There was a relevant paper he'd been reading, but he'd given up on it. He'd just read it through again, see if it was any less impenetrable now than it had been last night.

Not much, he realised a while later. He was too tired to concentrate, and the grammar was so convoluted it didn't make sense, no matter how many times he read it.

He needed to go to bed—but that meant facing Lucy, and the last thing he needed tonight was to have his head ripped off. Even if it was deserved. Dammit, there was a note on his phone, and it was in his diary. How could he have overlooked it?

And would it have made any difference, in the end? There'd been no one to cover the shift when the locum booked for it had rung in sick, and he'd had to twist his own registrar's arm to get him to come in at midnight and take over.

He let out a heavy sigh, gave the dog a biscuit in his bed and headed up the stairs with all the enthusiasm of a French nobleman heading for the guillotine.

She'd heard the crunch of gravel under tyres, heard the garage door slide open and closed, heard the murmur of his voice as he talked to the dog. And then silence.

He'd gone into the study, she realised, peering out of the bedroom window and seeing the spill of light across the drive.

Why hadn't he come to bed?

Guilt?

Indifference?

It could have been either, because he surely wasn't *still* working. She felt the crushing weight of sadness overwhelm her. She didn't know him any more. It was like living with a stranger. He hardly spoke, all his utterances monosyllabic, and the dry wit which had been his trademark seemed to have been wiped away since Lottie's birth.

And she couldn't do it any more.

She heard the stairs creak, and turned on her side away from him. She heard the bathroom door close, water running, the click of the light switch as he came out then felt the mattress dip slightly.

'Luce?'

His voice came softly to her in the darkness, deep and gruff, the word slightly slurred with tiredness.

She bit her lip. She wasn't going to do this, wasn't going to let him try and win her round. She knew what would happen if she spoke. He'd apologise, nuzzle her neck, kiss her, and then her traitorous body would forgive him everything and the moment would be lost, swept under the carpet as usual.

Well, not this time. This time they were going to talk about it.

Tomorrow. Without fail.

He lay beside her in the silence of the night, listening to the quiet, slightly uneven sound of her breathing.

She wasn't asleep. He knew that, but he wasn't going to push it. He was too tired to be reasonable, and they'd end up having an almighty row and flaying each other to shreds.

Except they hadn't even done that recently.

They hadn't done anything much together recently, and he couldn't remember the last time he'd made love to her.

Weeks ago?

Months?

No. Surely not months.

He was too tired to work it out, but the hollow ache of regret in his chest was preventing him from sleeping, and he lay there, staring at the ghostly white moonlight filtering round the edge of the curtains, until exhaustion won and he finally fell asleep.

* * *

'Did he come home?'

'Not until very, very late,' she told Emily. 'Here, eat your toast. Megan's had hers.'

She painstakingly spread butter onto the toast, then stuck the buttery knife into the chocolate spread and smeared it on the toast, precisely edge to edge, her tongue sticking slightly out of the side of her mouth in concentration. When it was all done to her satisfaction, she looked up and said, 'So didn't you go at all? Even later?'

'No. It doesn't matter.'

'Yes, it does, Mummy. He broke a promise!'

She blinked away the tears and hugged her daughter. Their daughter. So like her father—the floppy dark hair, the slate blue eyes, the tilt of her lips—everything. Megan with her light brown curls and clear green eyes was the image of her mother, but Emily and Lottie were little clones of Andy, and just looking at them broke her heart.

Em was so straightforward, so honest and kind and loving, everything she'd fallen for in Andy. But now...

'Where is he? Is he still sleeping?'

'I think so. He came to bed very late, so I left him. What do you want to do today?'

'Something with Daddy.'

'Can we feed the ducks?' Megan asked, glancing up from the dog's bed where she was curled up with Stanley gently pulling his ears up into points. The patient dog loved Megan, and tolerated almost anything. 'Stanley likes to feed the ducks.'

'Only because you give him the bread,' she said drily. 'Yes, we can feed the ducks.'

'I'll go and wake Daddy up,' Emily said, jumping down off her chair and sprinting for the stairs.

'Em, no! Leave him to sleep—'

But it was too late. She heard voices on the landing, and

realised Andy must already be up. The stairs creaked, and her heart began to thump a little harder, the impending confrontation that had been eating at her all night rearing its ugly head over the breakfast table.

'Daddy, you have to say sorry to Mummy because you broke a promise,' Em said, towing him into the kitchen, and Lucy looked up and met his stony gaze and her heart sank.

'I had no choice. Didn't Mummy explain that to you? She should have done. I can't leave people to die, Em, promise or not. That's my biggest promise, and it has to come first.'

'Then you shouldn't have promised Mummy.'

'I would have thought our marriage vows were your biggest promise,' Lucy said softly, and he felt a knife twist in his heart.

'Don't go there, Luce. That isn't fair.'

'Isn't it?'

His glance flicked over the children warningly, and she nodded. 'Girls, go and get washed and dressed.'

'Are we feeding the ducks?'

'Yes,' Lucy said, and they pelted for the door.

'I want to carry the bread—'

'No, you give it all to Stanley—'

'*Are* we feeding the ducks?' he asked when their thundering footsteps had receded, and she shrugged.

'I don't know. I am, and they are. Are you going to deign to join us?'

'Luce, that's bloody unfair—'

'No, it's not. You're bloody unfair. And don't swear in front of Lottie.'

He clamped his teeth together on the retort and turned to the kettle.

'For heaven's sake, Lucy, you're being totally unreasonable. I didn't have a choice, I let you know, I apologised—'

'So that's all right, is it? You apologised, so it makes it

all OK? What about our marriage vows, Andy? Don't they mean anything to you any more? Don't I mean anything? Don't we? Us, you and me, and the children we've had together? Because right now it doesn't feel like it. It feels like we no longer have a marriage.'

He turned and stared at her as if she was mad. 'Of course we do,' he said, his voice slightly impatient as if her faculties were impaired. 'It's just a rough time. We're ridiculously understaffed at work till James gets back, and I'm trying to get this assignment done, but it doesn't mean there's anything wrong with our marriage.'

'Doesn't it? Just sleeping here for a few hours a night doesn't qualify as marriage, Andy. Being here, wanting to be here—that's a marriage, not taking every shift that's going and filling your life with one academic exercise after another just so you can avoid us!'

'Now you're really being ridiculous! I don't have time for this—'

'No, of course you don't, that would involve talking to me, having a conversation! And we all know you won't do that!'

He stalked off, shut the study door firmly and left her there fuming, the subject once again brushed aside.

He watched them go, listened to the girls' excited chatter, the dog whining until the door was opened, then trotting beside Lucy and the buggy while the girls dashed ahead, pausing obediently on the edge of the pavement.

They went out of the gate and turned right, and Lucy glanced back over her shoulder. She couldn't see him, he was standing at the back of the study with Emily's words ringing in his ears, but he could read the disappointment and condemnation in her eyes.

He'd been about to go out into the hall, to say he'd go with them, but then he'd heard Em ask if he was coming.

'No,' Lucy had replied. 'He's too busy.'

'He's *always* too busy,' Emily had said, her voice sad and resigned, and he'd felt it slice right through him.

He should have gone out into the hall there and then and said he was joining them. It wasn't too late even now, he could pull his boots on and catch up, they wouldn't have got far.

But he didn't. He really, really had to finish this assignment today, so he watched them out of sight, and then he went into the kitchen, put some toast in, switched the kettle on again and made a pot of coffee. His hand shook slightly as he poured the water onto the grounds, and he set the kettle down abruptly.

Stress. It must be stress. And no wonder.

He tipped his head back and let out a long, shaky sigh. God, he'd got some work to do to make up for this. Em's voice echoed in his head. *Daddy, you broke a promise.* After all he'd said to them, everything he believed in, and he'd let them down. Lucy should have explained to them, but frankly it didn't sound as if she herself understood.

Well, she ought to. She was a doctor, too, a GP—or she had been until they'd had Lottie. She was still on maternity leave, debating going back again part time as she had before, just a couple of sessions a week.

He didn't want her to go back, thought the children needed her more than they needed the money, and it was yet another bone of contention. They seemed to be falling over them all the time, these bones.

The skeleton of their marriage?

He pressed the plunger and poured the coffee, buttered his toast with Emily's knife and then pulled a face at the streak of chocolate spread smeared in with the butter. He drowned it out with bitter marmalade, and sat staring out at the bedraggled and windswept garden.

He couldn't remember when they'd last been out there doing anything together. June, maybe, when Lottie was three months old? He'd mowed the lawn from time to time, but they hadn't cut the perennials down yet for the winter, or trimmed back the evergreens, or cleared the summer pots and tubs. Lucy had been preoccupied with Lottie, and he'd been too busy to do anything other than go to work, come home to eat and then shut himself in the study until he was too tired to work any longer. If he'd made it into the sitting room so he could be with Lucy, he'd had the laptop so he could carry on working until he fell into bed.

He must have been mad taking on the course, but it was nearly done now, this one last assignment the finish of it. That, and the exam he had to sit in a fortnight. Lord knows when he'd find time to revise for that. Lucy was taking the kids away to her parents for half term to give him some time to concentrate, but he knew it wouldn't be enough, not if he was at work all day. And there was still this blasted assignment to knock on the head.

Refilling his mug, he took his coffee back into the study, shut the door and had another go at making sense of that overly wordy and meaningless paper.

Or maybe he should just ignore it and press on without referring to it. Then he could finish the assignment off this morning, and tonight he could take Lucy out and try and make it up to her.

Good idea.

'Don't cook for us, I'm taking you out for dinner.'

Lucy looked at him as if he was mad. 'Have you got a babysitter?'

'Not yet.'

'Well, good luck with that. Anyway, I don't want to go out for dinner.'

He stared at her, stunned. He'd bust a gut finishing off the assignment so he could spare the time, and now this? 'Why ever not? You like going out for dinner.'

'Not when we're hardly speaking! It's not my idea of fun to sit opposite you while you're lost in thought on some stupid assignment or other for a course you've taken on without consulting me—'

'Well, what *do* you want to do?'

'I don't want to *do* anything! I want you to *talk* to me! I want you to share decisions, not just steam ahead and do your own thing and leave us all behind! I want you to put the kids to bed, read them a story, give me a hug, bring me a cup of tea. I don't need extravagant gestures, Andy, I just need *you* back.'

He sighed shortly, ramming his hand through his hair. 'I haven't gone anywhere, Lucy. I'm doing this for all of us.'

'Are you? Well, it doesn't feel like it. It feels like you're just shutting us out, as if we don't matter as much as your blasted career—'

'That's unfair.'

'No, it isn't! You're unfair. Neglecting your children is unfair. When did you last put Lottie to bed?'

He swallowed hard and turned away. 'Luce, it's been chaos—'

'Don't give me excuses!'

'It's not an excuse, it's a reason,' he said tautly. 'Anyway, I'm around tomorrow. We'll do something then, all of us.'

'Are you sure? You aren't going to find something else to do?'

'No! I'm here. All day. I promise.'

'And I'm supposed to believe that?'

'Oh, for God's sake, I haven't got time for this. I've got work to do—'

'Of course you have. You always have work to do, and it's always more important than us. I don't know what the hell's wrong with you.'

This time she was the one who walked off. She shouldered past him, went into the utility room, shut the door firmly and started to tackle the ironing while Lottie was napping.

His phone rang just before eleven that night, while he was printing off the hated assignment. HR? Really?

Really.

'Oh, you're kidding, Steve! Not again.'

'Sorry, Andy. There isn't anyone else. James isn't back in the country until tomorrow, or I'd ask him. It's just one of those things. I'll sort a new locum first thing on Monday, I promise.'

He gave a heavy sigh and surrendered. 'All right—but this is the last time, Steve. And you owe me, with bells on.'

He hung up, and sat there for a while wondering how on earth he was going to tell Lucy. She'd skin him alive.

And deservedly so.

He swore softly but succinctly under his breath, stacked the papers together, clipped them into a binder and put the assignment into an envelope without even glancing at it. It was too late to worry. It had to be there on Monday, and it was already too late to post it. He'd email it, but the hard copy would have to be couriered.

He'd do that on Monday morning, but now he was working all day tomorrow there was no time for any meaningful read-through before he sent it on its way. He'd only find some howler and, frankly, at this moment in time it seemed insignificant compared to telling Lucy that yet again he wasn't going to be there for any quality time with her and the kids.

It was *not* a conversation he was looking forward to.

She was asleep by the time he went upstairs, and he got into bed beside her and contemplated pulling her into his arms and making love to her.

Probably not a good idea. He didn't have the energy to do her justice and he had to be at work in seven hours. Cursing Steve and the sick locum and life in general, he shut his eyes, covered them with his arm and crashed into sleep.

The alarm on his phone woke him long before he was ready for it, and he silenced it and got straight out of bed before he could fall asleep again. Hell, he was tired. He stumbled into the bathroom, turned on the shower and got in without waiting for it to heat up.

The cold shocked him awake, and he soaped himself fast, towelled his body briskly and then ran the razor over his jaw. His hand was trembling again, he noticed, and he nicked himself.

Damn. It was the last thing he needed. He dried his face, leaving a bright streak of blood on the towel, and pressed a scrap of tissue over the cut to stem the bleeding while he cleaned his teeth.

He went back into the bedroom, leaving the bathroom door open so he could see to get his clothes out without putting on the bedroom light. He didn't want to disturb Lucy—because he was hoping to sneak out without waking her? Probably, but it was too late for that, apparently.

'Andy?' she murmured, her voice soft with sleep. 'Are you OK?'

Was he? Frankly, he had no idea. He pulled clothes out of the cupboard and started putting them on, and she propped herself up on one elbow and stared at him.

'What are you doing, Andy? It's Sunday morning. We don't need to get up yet.'

'I have to work. Steve rang last night, and I promised to do another shift—'

'No! Why?' She shoved herself up in the bed, dishevelled and sleepy and so beautiful she made his heart ache, her eyes filled with recrimination and disappointment. 'Andy, you *promised* me! Why on earth did you agree? We don't need the money, but we need *you*. The kids need you. *I* need you.'

'And the hospital needs me—'

'So put it first. Again. As always. Go on, go ahead—if that's more important to you than us.'

'Of course it's not more important!'

'Then don't *go*!'

'I *have* to! There's nobody to cover the department.'

'So they'll have to shut it.'

'They can't. They can't close the ED, Lucy, you're being totally unreasonable.'

'Well, you know what you can do, then. Go, by all means, but don't bother coming home tonight, or any other night, because I can't do this any more.'

He stared at her, slightly stunned. 'Is that an ultimatum?'

'Sounds like it to me.'

'Oh, Lucy, for heaven's sake, that's ridiculous! You can't make me choose!'

'I don't need to. Strikes me you already have. You come home after the children are asleep, you leave before they're up—and when you're here in the evening, you're shut in your study or sitting behind your laptop screen totally ignoring me! What exactly do you think you're bringing to this relationship?'

'The money?' he said sarcastically, and her face drained of colour.

'You arrogant bastard,' she spat softly. 'We don't need your money, and we certainly don't need your attitude. I can go back to work for more days. I'm going back anyway next month for three sessions a week. They've asked me to, and I've said yes, and Lottie's going to nursery. I'll just do more hours, more sessions. They want as much time as I can give them, so I'll give them more, if that's what it takes.'

He stared at her, shocked. 'When did they ask you? You didn't tell me.'

'When exactly was I supposed to tell you?' she asked, her voice tinged with bitterness and disappointment. 'You're never here.'

'That's not true. I was here all day yesterday—'

'Shut in your study doing something more important!'

'Don't be silly. This is important. You should have told me. You don't need to go back to work.'

'Yes, I do! I need to because if I don't, I never get to have a sensible conversation with another adult, because you certainly aren't around! You have no idea what it's like talking to a seven month old baby all day, every day, with no relief from it except for the conversation of her seven and five year old sisters! I love her to bits, I love them all to bits, but I'm not just a mother, I'm a doctor, I'm a woman, and those parts of me need recognition. And they're sure as hell not getting them from you!'

He sucked in his breath, stung by the bitterness in her voice. 'Luce, that's not fair. I'm doing it for us—'

'No, you're not! You're doing it for you, for your precious ego that demands you never say no, always play the hero, always step up to the plate and never let your patients down. But you're a husband and a father as well as a doctor, and you're just sweeping all that under the mat. Well, newsflash, Gallagher, I'm not going to be swept under the mat any more. I don't need the scraps of you left over from your "real" life, and nor do your children. We can manage without you. We do most of the time anyway. I doubt we'll even notice the difference.'

He felt sick. 'You don't mean that. Where will you live?'

'Here?' she shrugged. 'I can take over the mortgage.'

'What, on a part-time salary? Dream on, Lucy.'

'So we'll move. It doesn't matter. All that matters is that we're happy, and we're not at the moment, so go. Go to your precious hospital if you really must, but you have to realise that if you do, you won't have a marriage to come back to, not even a lousy one.'

He stared at her, at the distress and anger and challenge in her eyes, and, for the briefest moment, he hesitated. Then, because he really had no choice, he turned on his heel and walked out of their bedroom and down the stairs.

She'd cool off. He'd give her time to think about it, time to consider all they'd be losing, and after he finished work, he'd come home and apologise, bring her some flowers and chocolates and a bottle of wine. Maybe a takeaway so she didn't have to cook.

And he'd make love to her, long and slow, and she'd forgive him.

Two more weeks, he told himself grimly. Just two more weeks until the course was finished and the exam was over, and then they could sort this out.

They'd be fine. It was just a rocky patch, everyone had them. They'd deal with it.

He scooped up his keys, shrugged on his jacket and left.

CHAPTER TWO

HE'D gone. Turned on his heel and walked out.

She'd heard the utility room door close, the garage door slide up, the car start. Slightly open-mouthed with shock, she'd sat there in their bed, the quilt fisted in her hands, and listened to the shreds of their marriage disappearing off the drive in a slew of gravel.

The silence that followed was deafening.

She couldn't believe he'd gone. She'd thought—

What? That he'd stay? That he'd phone the hospital and tell them he couldn't go in, his wife had thrown a strop and threatened to kick him out? Hardly. It wasn't Andy's style. If he didn't talk to her, he sure as eggs didn't talk to anyone else.

And he'd told Steve he'd do it, so it was set in stone. It seemed that everything except them was set in stone.

She felt a sob rising in her throat, but she crushed it ruthlessly. This wasn't the time for tears. She had the children to think about. Later, maybe, after they were in bed again, she'd cry. For now, she could hear Lottie chatting in her cot, and she pushed the covers aside and swung her legs over the edge of the bed, heading for her baby on autopilot.

She'd pack him some clothes—just enough to tide him over, give him time to think about things—and drop them off at work. Maybe that would shock him to his senses, because something surely had to.

She walked into Lottie's room, into the sunshine of her smile, and felt grief slam into her chest. What had their baby done to deserve this?

'Hello, my precious,' she crooned softly. 'Oh, you're so gorgeous—come here.' She scooped the beaming baby up against her heart and hugged her tight. Delicious, darling child, she thought, aching for what was to come. The fall-out from this didn't bear thinking about.

But Lottie didn't know and she didn't care. She was beginning to whine now, pulling at Lucy's top, and she took her back to bed and fed her.

She was still breastfeeding her night and morning, but she might not be able to keep it going, she realised with a sick feeling in the pit of her stomach, not if she had to get the girls ready for school and out of the door in time to get to work. She stared down, watching her daughter suckle, treasuring every second of this fleeting, precious moment.

The baby flung her little arm out, turning her head at a sound from the window, endlessly curious and distracted now her thirst was slaked, and Lucy sat her up in the middle of the bed and handed her a toy to play with while she packed a bag for Andy.

It seemed so wrong—so unnecessary! Why couldn't he see? Why couldn't he give them the time they surely deserved?

Damn. She swallowed the tears down, threw his razor and deodorant and toothbrush into a washbag, tucked it into the holdall and zipped it up. There. Done. She'd drop it in later, on their way out somewhere.

The zoo?

No. It was cold and rainy. Maybe she'd take them swimming to the leisure centre, to take their minds off Andy's absence.

Oh, help. She'd have to tell the girls something—but what?

That he was working? So busy working he didn't have time to come home, so he was going to stay at the hospital?

That was a good point. She had no idea where he'd stay, and she told herself she didn't care, but he might need to wear something at night. She unzipped the bag again, put in the emergency pyjamas which never saw the light of day and a clean dressing gown and the slippers his aunt had sent him for Christmas last year, and tugged the zip closed with a sinking feeling.

Christmas. It was only a little over two months away.

Would he be there with them for Christmas? What if he never came to his senses?

What if they simply didn't matter that much to him?

She choked down the sob and scooped Lottie up, carrying her and the holdall downstairs and putting her in the high chair with some toys while she put the bag into her car. He'd need his laptop, she realised, and went into his study to get it. She wasn't giving him an excuse to come back here tonight and try to win her round. They'd been married ten years now and she knew how his mind worked. No. He had to take this seriously.

There was a large brown envelope lying on the lid of his laptop, the address written in his bold, slashing script. His assignment, she realised. She frowned at it. His writing was untidier than usual—because he was so tired? Probably. His fault, she told herself, crushing the little flicker of sympathy.

She put the envelope into the case with the computer, threw in the power lead and his flash drive, then remembered his mobile phone charger, as well, and took the case out to the garage.

By the time she got back into the kitchen, the girls were coming down the stairs, giggling and chasing each other into the kitchen.

Oh, lord, how to tell them?

'Morning, darlings.'

'Morning!' Emily reached up as she bent down and kissed her, then went and sat at the table, legs swinging. 'Mummy, what are we doing today?'

Megan's arms were round her hips hugging her, and she stroked her hair automatically and tried to smile at her daughters. 'I don't know. What would you like to do?'

'Can we feed the ducks with Daddy?' Megan asked, tipping her head back, her eyes pleading.

She hauled in a breath, her smile faltering. 'No, sorry, he's had to go to work.'

'But he said he wasn't working today!' Emily said, looking appalled. 'He *promised* us!'

'I know. He didn't want to go but they didn't have anyone else. And he can't let people suffer.'

The words had a hollow ring of truth, but she brushed them aside. He *could* have said no. They would have found someone, or if necessary closed the unit. Or he could at least have talked to her about it, instead of presenting it as a *fait accompli*.

'Actually, he's going to be so busy he's going to stay at the hospital for a few nights,' she said, the lie sticking in her throat. 'So, anyway, I thought maybe we could go swimming after breakfast. What do you think? And then maybe we can get pizza for lunch.'

Their replies sounded fairly enthusiastic, but there was something missing, some extra sparkle and fizz, another dimension that should have been there.

Andy. Their father, her husband, the man who broke promises.

Don't go there!

'Right. Who wants what for breakfast?'

It was tedious and chaotic and half the people didn't need to be there.

Realistically, they could have got anyone to cover him, he thought grimly as he worked his way through the sprains and strains and fractures that yesterday's sporting fixtures had left in their wake. It was all basic stuff, the sort of thing that any half-decent doctor could deal with, and the thought made him angry.

'Right, you'll need to come to the Fracture Clinic tomorrow morning between eight and nine for assessment and a proper cast. Here's a prescription for pain relief.'

He scrawled his signature on the bottom, handed it over and walked out, shaking his head and rolling it on his neck. It ached, and he couldn't think clearly. He was so, so tired. Maybe Lucy was right. Maybe he should have just said no, and they would have had to close the unit. That might have made them sit up and take notice and get a bit better organised.

In the meantime, he needed a coffee. A strong one.

'Oh, Mr Gallagher, your wife dropped your case and laptop off. They're behind here,' the receptionist said as he passed her.

He stared at her for a shocked half-second, then nodded. 'Yes—of course. Sorry, miles away. Could you stick them in my office?'

'Sure.' She eyed him thoughtfully. 'Mr Gallagher, are you OK?'

'I'm fine, Jane. I'm just tired,' he muttered, and then went behind reception. 'Actually I'll take them myself,' he said, and hoisting the bag and laptop case up, he headed for his office.

He could feel her eyes boring into him all the way, hear the speculation starting. Damn Lucy! Damn her for making it all so much worse than it had to be.

He shut the door, dumped the bags on the floor behind his desk and slammed his fist down on it.

How *dare* she! How dare she bring his things in like that and make a public spectacle of their dirty laundry?

He pulled his phone out of his pocket and speed-dialled her number. It went straight to answerphone. Screening his call?

'I've just been accosted by a curious receptionist who handed me an overnight bag,' he said shortly. 'What the hell do you think you're playing at? Call me!'

He cut the connection and threw the phone down on the desk in disgust.

She'd meant it. She'd really, really meant it.

He felt numb, and slightly sick. And homeless? Where was he going to stay?

Stupid. He should just go home, have it out with her, make a few promises—*and keep them*, his conscience prodded—and deal with it. Except he was angry—angry with Steve for asking him to cover again, angry with the whole locum situation, angry with Lucy for not being reasonable, but most of all angry with himself for letting it all get out of hand by not saying no. Not to mention taking on the course, which was the just the last straw on the back of this failing camel that was their marriage.

And it wasn't going to get any better until the course was over, until he'd sat the exam and could put the whole damn thing to bed. Then he could go back to Lucy and talk about this.

And in the meantime, they could have a cooling off

period. Lucy could calm down a bit, so could he, and he could shut himself away somewhere and work so he had the slightest chance of passing the course, to make the whole thing worthwhile.

It was half term next week and Lucy had already arranged to take the children to her parents so he could revise in peace. So he'd check into a hotel, get the exam out of the way and then they could all get back to normal.

But first, they needed to agree on what they were telling the children, because the last thing he wanted was them thinking that their marriage was coming to an end when it wasn't—or at least, not if he had anything to say about it.

He pulled the telephone directory out of his drawer, looked up the number of a decent hotel chain which had a motel nearby and booked himself a room.

And then he went back to work, asked one of the nurses to bring him back a coffee when she came back from her break and took the next set of notes out of the rack.

The receptionist gave him a wide berth for the rest of the day.

He wasn't surprised. Gossip travelled like wildfire through hospitals, and even though there was nothing to know, really, he could sense the speculation.

He hated it. Hated that they were talking about him behind his back, hated that when he walked out at the end of the day carrying his bag and laptop case, he could feel eyes following him.

You're imagining it, he told himself, throwing the cases in the car and slamming the boot, still furious with Lucy. The motel was just a couple of minutes away, on the road into town, and he checked in and went straight to his room.

Clean, functional, with a kingsize bed, a sofa, a desk with a work light and a bathroom with a decent power shower, it was the generic hotel room. Everything he needed, but soulless and empty, because the only thing he really needed was his family.

His throat felt tight, and he swallowed hard and dumped the bags on the bed. She still hadn't called him. Why not? It was six o'clock. She'd be dealing with the children.

Fine. He'd go over to the indifferent restaurant, get himself something to eat and then come back here and work, otherwise this whole damn fiasco would be pointless.

She stared at the phone, her lip caught between her teeth, and psyched herself up to call him.

He was right. She shouldn't have dumped his stuff in reception. She'd been steaming mad with him, but she could as easily have put it in the boot of his car and sent him a text.

She owed him an apology for that, and he was right, they needed to talk about the children, to arrange a time for him to see them so they didn't feel cut off from him. That was the last thing she wanted.

Sucking in a deep breath, she dialled his number, and he answered on the first ring.

'This better be good, Lucy.'

'I'm sorry,' she said, before he could get another word in. 'I didn't think. I was just cross. Andy, we need to talk.'

'Yes, we do. You don't just kick me out like a damn cat and then publicly humiliate me in front of the entire department. You owe me more than that, whatever beef you might have with me. And you owe the kids more. They're at school with other staff members' children, and you know what hospitals are like, so what story are we coming up with so they don't end up being screwed over by this nonsense?'

'It isn't nonsense, Andy. Our marriage is foundering, and you have to start taking that seriously.'

'Oh, I take it seriously. Very seriously. I also take my job seriously, but the kids come first, even if it doesn't seem like it, and right now, I'm being pulled in so many directions I can't be reasonable about this. Of all the times to pick—'

'It's because of this time!' she interrupted. 'Precisely *because* of what's been going on! And that blasted course—'

'I don't want the children thinking there's a rift in our marriage, not until we've tried and failed to work it out, and I don't want that to happen under any circumstances, but I can't deal with this now. I'll do what you say, I'll keep out of the way, get this exam over and the course finished, and then we'll talk, but play fair and cut me some slack, Luce, because I'm so tired I'm at breaking point.'

His voice cracked, and she swallowed a sob. She nearly told him to come home, but what he said made sense.

'OK. We'll do that. I've told the children you're so busy at the hospital that you're going to stay there for a few days. We'll stick with that. I'm away with them next week anyway, so you can work undisturbed. And then after the exam, we'll talk about this. OK?'

He gave a ragged sigh. 'OK. I'll come round tomorrow night and see them for a few minutes.'

Her heart hitched, but she had no choice, and he was right. 'OK. Want supper?'

'No. And don't tell them, just in case I get held up. I don't want to break any more promises to anyone, so it's easier if I don't make them.'

Her eyes filled, and she nodded. 'All right. Well—get here if you can.'

'I will. And—oh, nothing. Doesn't matter. I'll see you tomorrow.'

The phone went dead, and she stared at it. What had he been going to say?

I love you?

Unlikely. He hadn't said it for ages. A year, maybe? She couldn't remember, it was so long ago.

She pressed her hand to her mouth, but the sob wouldn't stay down, so she buried her face in a cushion to stifle the sound and wept for the man she loved and might have lost...

He finished on time on Monday, by a miracle, so he could get home in time to see the children. He needed some things from the study and a few more clothes, as well, and he wanted to see the children so much it made him ache inside. They hadn't asked for any of this, and he didn't see why they should suffer.

Lucy's car was still on the drive, and he pulled up beside it and headed for the front door. As he slid his key into the keyhole he wondered fleetingly if she would have changed the locks.

No. The key turned, the door swung quietly open and Stanley was there to greet him, tail lashing, tongue lolling in delight.

'Hello, boy,' he said gruffly, and then Emily was in the hall, looking pleased to see him but a bit wary, and it nearly broke his heart.

'Mummy said you weren't coming home this week,' she said, hanging back a little. 'She said you were too busy and you were going to stay at the hospital.'

Oh, Em. He ushered her back into the kitchen where Lucy was wiping supper off Lottie's face and hair and arms.

'Well, they finally got a locum so I finished early,' he said truthfully, 'so I thought I'd come and see you all for a few minutes and pick up some stuff. And I'm really sorry about yesterday.'

'Are you staying here tonight now, then?' Megan asked innocently, and he glanced up and met Lucy's guarded but feisty eyes and smiled grimly.

'No, darling, I'm sorry, I've got to go back to work. So, what did you guys do yesterday?' he asked, suddenly desperately sorry that he'd missed it. 'Did you have fun?'

'Mummy took us swimming, and Florence was there,' Megan said, 'and we all went swimming together.'

'Florence?' he asked.

'Ben Walker's daughter. She's in Megan's class,' Lucy filled in, and he nodded. He knew Ben. He was an obstetrician, and he'd met little Florence when she'd dislocated her elbow a couple of years ago. He'd married his registrar, Daisy, and they'd had a baby since. They were a nice family. Happy. Stable. Unlike them...

'And Daisy was there, and Thomas, and Daisy's going to have a new baby soon!' Emily said. 'And then we went for pizza, because Florence's Daddy was at the hospital, too, and Mummy and Daisy are going for coffee tomorrow after we go to school. And it's not fair, 'cos they'll have cake, and I want cake,' she added mournfully.

He found himself smiling, despite the ache lodged solidly behind his sternum. 'Sounds like you had a good day,' he said, but Megan was hugging his legs and tugging at him for attention.

'Please can you read us a story?' she asked, her pleading eyes shredding him.

He shook his head, wishing he could but there just wasn't time, not if he was going to get any work done. 'No. Sorry. I have to sort some things out and then get back, but I will one night soon.'

Her face fell, tearing another strip off his heart, and she gazed sadly up at him. 'When, Daddy?'

Always questions. Questions that demanded answers that nearly always seemed to be promises destined to be broken.

'Soon,' he said again, knowing it was meaningless but unwilling to make another promise that fate could so easily break, and he hugged her, pressing a kiss to her toffee-coloured curls and letting go. Emily trailed him into the study and stood watching while he searched for a memory stick with some information on it he needed, and in the background he could hear Lottie crying tiredly and Megan crooning to her while Lucy cleared up the kitchen.

'Why can't you stay here and work?' Em asked, squiggling one toe on the floor, her leg swinging from side to side rhythmically as she watched him. 'You always do.'

'It's not that sort of work,' he lied, and felt a wave of resentment that Lucy was bringing them all to this. His fingers closed around the memory stick and he pulled it out and shut the drawer. 'Got it. Right, sweetheart, I need to head off. You be good for Mummy, OK?'

'I'm always good,' she said reproachfully, and he hugged her, because it was true, she was a good girl and he loved her more than he could ever find the words.

'It's not for long,' he said, mentally crossing his fingers as he bent to kiss her goodnight. 'I'll see you again in a day or two.'

'Ring first,' Lucy said from the doorway. She was standing there with Lottie, and the baby was leaning out towards him and grizzling, so he took her and hugged her tight, crushing the lump in his throat and gritting his teeth.

'I'd better go,' he said, handing Lottie back and ruffling Megan's hair. 'I'll see you soon, guys.'

He let himself out, shutting the door behind him without collecting any of the clothes he'd meant to get, and all the way back to the motel he wrestled with the lump in his throat.

'Right, where are we going for coffee?'

Coffee?

Lucy stared at Daisy, then shut her eyes. 'Sorry, I'd forgotten. It's been a bit…'

She bit her lip and looked away, and Daisy tutted and started to walk. 'Come on, we'll go back to mine. Ben bought some really nice coffee, and I made chocolate brownies yesterday. Sometimes a girl just needs chocolate.'

Lucy hesitated for a split second, then went with her. Ben and Daisy had moved recently to a lovely Victorian house a couple of streets away. She'd been itching to see it, but now, suddenly, it didn't seem important any more. Nothing did, apart from Andy, but Daisy's kindness called out to her, and she knew instinctively that anything she said would stay right there and she so needed a friend to talk to.

'What about the buggy?' she asked as Daisy opened the battered but beautiful old front door. 'The wheels are a bit muddy but Lottie's asleep.'

'Oh, you're fine. The floor's tiled. Bring her in.'

Daisy let Thomas out of his buggy and headed for the kitchen, and Lucy left Lottie sleeping and followed her, staring around at the shabby, tatty grandeur of the lovely old house.

'Excuse the mess, we've got quite a lot to do here,' Daisy said with a grin, reaching for the kettle, then her smile softened. 'Sit down and relax. You look shattered, Lucy.'

She sat, unwilling to talk about the mess her marriage was in and yet so desperate to pour it all out, to share the craziness that was her life right now.

Daisy put a cake tin on the table, plonked the cafetière

down beside it with a couple of mugs and a jug of foamed hot milk, then sat Thomas in his high chair with a drink and a chunk of squidgy, gooey chocolate cake that Lucy just knew would go everywhere, but Daisy didn't seem to care in the least.

'Right,' she said, settling down and smiling at Lucy. 'Coffee?'

She let her breath out on a little huff and smiled. 'Please. That would be lovely. And some of that. It looks really good.'

Daisy put the coffee down in front of her, handed her chocolate sprinkles and a massive chunk of brownie and then stirred her coffee thoughtfully.

'Lucy, I don't want to invade your privacy,' she said gently after a pregnant silence, 'but—if you want to unload, it won't go any further, and I can see something's wrong. Is there anything I can do to help?'

'Do?' she asked, staring at Daisy and seeing concern in her eyes. They swam out of focus, and she looked quickly away. 'I wish. We're just—Andy's really busy, and he's been working stupid hours, and…'

'And?' Daisy prompted gently, and the floodgates opened.

'They asked him to work on Sunday and he said yes, but he'd promised the kids he'd do something with them and I just flipped.'

'Everyone needs a good row now and then,' Daisy said pragmatically.

'But it wasn't a good row,' she said, remembering the bitterness, the acrimony, the stubborn thrust of his jaw. 'That would have been fine. This—this was an awful row, and I told him to go. I thought—I was just calling his bluff, but he went. He just—went. And I let him go, Daisy,' she said, swiping at her nose because it was suddenly running and her eyes were welling and there was a sob just itching to get out if she'd only let it.

'Oh, Lucy…'

Daisy wrapped her hand in hers and squeezed, and the simple gesture pushed Lucy over the brink. She felt the tears well over and splash down her cheeks, but she couldn't stop them, and with a muffled murmur Daisy hugged her gently and let her cry, then shoved a tissue in her hand and let her talk.

'He just doesn't seem the same. I know it sounds crazy, but I feel as if I don't know him any more. He's not who he was—and it's since Lottie. I thought he wanted another baby, but ever since she was born he's been really strange—distant, distracted, as if we aren't really there half the time. And he's got the most amazing sense of humour normally. He's so funny, so sharp, and that's just gone. It's like living with a stranger.'

'Ben said the ED's been bedlam since James went on holiday, and I gather the maternity leave locum's been a bit flaky.'

'Flaky? Try downright skiving. She's never there. That's why I wasn't at book club on Friday night. And instead of saying they should shut the department and send everyone to another ED, Andy just takes another shift, and then another one, and they walk all over him, because he can't just let people down, but the kids—'

She broke off, biting her lip, and Daisy sighed and topped up her coffee. 'Tough choices.'

'Impossible,' she went on. 'The nearest ED is miles away, and time is so important, but so is family. You're a doctor, you know what it's like, the hypocritical oath that tells you to put everyone before your own, so we always seem to come last.'

'Oh, tell me about it. I've threatened to kill Ben before

now, but I'm just as bad. We were in Theatre delivering some twins the night before our wedding, and I really wonder what would have happened if they'd needed us on our wedding night.'

Lucy smiled wryly. 'I do understand what it's like for him. I know how it is, but—I just feel, if I don't fight for our marriage, then who will? Not him, he didn't even realise it's going down the pan. And this stupid, stupid course he's taken on—really, I could kill him for that, because of all the unnecessary things…'

'What's it on?'

'Oh, I don't know. Something to do with stabilising patients with massive trauma—juggling acts, really. He gave me an assignment to proof-read the other week and I couldn't understand a word of it. And I'm a doctor.'

Daisy tipped her head on one side thoughtfully. 'Is he depressed?'

'Daisy, I have no idea. I don't think he's got time to be depressed, but he's exhausted, I know that, and Lottie's not going through the night properly yet, and I'm starting work again in two weeks, and I…'

'You're at your wits' end,' Daisy filled in gently. 'I can understand that. When's the course finish?'

'The exam's on Friday week, and then it's done. And James is back, and they had a new locum yesterday, Andy said, so maybe it'll sort itself out, once the pressure's off and we can all think straight. Well, that's what I'm hoping,' she added, and closed her eyes and sighed. 'Oh, I feel so disloyal talking to you about this—'

'Don't be stupid. You're just letting off steam. We all need to do it, and it won't go any further. And if there's anything I can do to help, just ask. Anything. The kids can stay over—whatever.'

'Oh, Daisy—that's so kind of you.'

'Rubbish. That's what friends are for. And since you're here, you can give me a hand. What do you think of this curtain fabric for the sitting room?'

It was a fortnight he could have done without, but at least the staffing crisis seemed to have been resolved now it was too late, he thought bitterly.

He went to the hospital, worked his shifts and no more, and every other evening he popped in and saw the children. Then Lucy, the girls and the dog went away to her parents for half term, he checked out of the hotel and went home, and he put his head down and worked until he was ready to drop.

And on the Friday of half term he went down to London to sit the exam, and he was so tired he could hardly answer the paper. He knew exactly what he wanted to say, but he just couldn't find the words, and he caught the train home kicking himself because it was all such a phenomenal waste of time. He'd have to re-sit it, he knew that, because he'd screwed up so badly on a couple of the questions, but in the meantime his marriage was on the rocks and he'd resorted to lying to his children.

And it looked as if it had all been for nothing.

CHAPTER THREE

THEY were due back from her parents' at lunchtime on Sunday. He was working until three, having swapped Friday with James, and then he was going home to see the children and hopefully talk to Lucy.

He had Monday off, and he'd thought they could spend the day together while the children were at school, but she was starting work at the practice that morning, apparently, so it was tonight or who knew when.

But first he had to get through the day, and it was another of those days. Cold, windy and as unpromising outside as it was in the department, and he was too tired to deal with it all.

Amongst the sports injuries and nose bleeds and dog bites was the inevitable night owl who'd sobered up and realised she'd hurt herself after falling off that table last night, and another who'd fallen down the stairs of a nightclub and fractured her skull and had only realised something was wrong this morning when she couldn't see straight.

They tried his patience, but it wasn't really their fault. He knew that, and it wasn't only them. There were the people who'd lain suffering all night and finally come in when the pain had become impossible to ignore. One was a query heart attack, another had an agonising kidney stone. He shunted them off to the appropriate departments, and then a gust of wind brought a tree down on a car, and an elderly woman with head injuries was brought in.

'Jean Darby, front seat passenger,' he was told. 'GCS thirteen at the scene, now ten, she's had oxygen and tramadol.'

'Is the driver on his way in?' he asked, trying not to worry about Lucy and the children out on the road in this weather, but the paramedic shook his head, his face filling in the details and ratcheting up the apprehension Andy was feeling.

He frowned and picked up her left hand. There were three rings on it—a wedding ring, an engagement ring and an eternity ring.

He stared at it. He still hadn't got Lucy the eternity ring he'd promised her when she was pregnant with Emily. Three babies later, she still didn't have it. Another item on that blasted list of ways in which he'd failed her. Failed all of them.

He put his family out of his mind and focused on the patient who'd very likely just lost her husband of many years. For now, she needed him. His family would be fine. They'd be home by now, and he'd see them later. Unlike this poor woman, who would never see her husband again, and might never see her family.

He knew how that would feel for them. He'd lost both his parents together in an accident, only a few years ago, and he'd felt reamed out inside.

He stroked her hand, squeezing it comfortingly.

'Hello, Jean. Can you hear me? You're in Yoxburgh Park Hospital. You've had an accident in the car.'

'Dennis,' she mumbled. 'Where's my husband? I need Dennis. Please find him...'

Her words were slurring worryingly. It might have been the drugs, but he didn't think so. She wasn't really responding, and he whipped out his pen light and shone it in her eyes. Sluggish pupils. Not good. His hand shook and he put the pen light back in his pocket.

'OK, Jean, just try and rest, he's in good hands. Will somebody contact CT and X-ray, please? We need a scan and a full head and neck series. And bloods. We'll need group and save, and—'

He stumbled, the familiar list eluding him, and he just waved a hand. 'Do a full set of bloods—all the usuals. And five minute obs, and get Neuro down here, Kazia. And someone contact the family, please. They need to be here now.'

Leaving the SHO in charge, he walked out, needing a break, a change of air—something. He had pins and needles in his hand now, and flashing lights.

A migraine? He'd had a few recently, although he hadn't mentioned it to anyone. Nothing major, just a bit of tingling for a few minutes. Painkillers, he thought, and went to find the sister in charge.

'Got a migraine. Any pills you can give me?'

'Sure. We'll have to write them up. What do you want?'

He tried to think of the drug names, and couldn't. 'Something strong,' he mumbled, and took them from her hand, his fingers shaking.

'Andy, are you OK?'

'I'm fine. Just tired and I've got a headache. I had that exam on Friday—I've been overdoing it.'

She looked at him sceptically, and he tried to smile, but it was all too much effort, so the moment he'd swallowed the pills he turned on his heel and walked back to Resus to see the woman.

Joan? Jane? He picked up the notes.

'Jean. How are you feeling?' he asked, but she didn't answer.

'I think she's got a bleed,' Kazia said softly, and he nodded.

'Um—Neuro on the way?'

'I'm here,' a familiar voice said from behind him, and he sighed with relief. He didn't need to deal with a junior, and nor did Jean.

'Raj, hi. Um—this is Jean—er—Darby—Kazia, would you fill us in?'

'Sure,' the SHO said, shooting him a strange look and taking over. He didn't mind. The words were escaping him, slithering away into the corners, hiding in the dark.

He propped himself against the Resus trolley and watched and listened as Raj ran through a quick neurological screen and then nodded.

'She needs to go to Theatre, but it's not looking good.'

It wasn't. In fact, it was considerably less than good, and that moment her pupils blew and she arrested. They worked on her, Andy doing chest compressions, Raj checking her pulse and haunting the monitor, but the odds were stacked hugely against her anyway, and after a few unsuccessful minutes Raj put his hands over Andy's and stopped him.

'This is pointless. She's gone, Andy.'

Damn. He straightened up and looked around, knowing he was right but gutted nonetheless. 'All agreed?' he asked, and everyone nodded.

He stared at the clock for an age, but he couldn't seem to get the words out. 'Time of death twelve thirty two,' he said after a long pause, and he stripped off his gloves, threw them in the bin and turned to the neurologist.

'Thanks, Raj. Sorry—waste of your time,' he said, his voice hitching slightly as if they were reluctant to come out, and Raj frowned and tipped his head on one side, searching his eyes.

'No problem. Got a minute?'

'Yeah, sure. Are the family here yet?'

'They're on their way.'

'OK. Find me when they're here. I want to see them.'

'Andy, now,' Raj said softly, and taking his elbow he steered him out of Resus, and then stopped in a quiet bit of the corridor. 'OK, what's going on? You're not yourself.'

'Don't know. I've got a migraine. Flashing lights, pins and needles—that sort of thing.'

'History?'

He shook his head. 'Not really. Bit. I've had a few in the last couple of months.'

'Have you been drinking?'

He shook his head. 'No. God, no. I'm just—tired.'

Raj took his hands. 'Squeeze.'

He squeezed, but even he could feel that his right hand wasn't working properly, and he felt his blood pressure kick up a notch as his heart started to pound. What the hell was wrong with him? The endless possibilities started spooling through his head, but he couldn't make sense of them.

'I think we need to take a proper look at you. Let's find somewhere quiet.'

He took him to a room reserved for patients kept in under observation, and laid him down, prodding and poking and shining lights in his pupils, making him count fingers and follow things with his eyes.

'What day is it?'

'Sunday, and I shouldn't be here, I should be with my kids.'

Raj smiled. 'I know the feeling. What's the time?'

He stared at the clock. 'Nearly ten past one.'

'Come on, I want more than that.'

'Thirteen oh eight,' he said after a second.

'Better. What do you give a child with anaphylaxis?'

'Um—' He swore, and looked away. 'Sorry. I can't...'

'Don't worry. Give me the words that go with these. Bread and…?'

'Butter.'

'Chalk and…?'

'Cheese.'

'What's the opposite of up?'

'Down.'

'And the opposite of accept?'

'Um—reject. Raj, what are you doing?' he asked, a bit shortly because, dammit, for a fraction of a second the word had eluded him.

'Trying to work out what's wrong with you, because something is and I don't think it's just migraine. I could be wrong, but I want you to have a scan. Shall we call Lucy?'

He felt a finger of fear creep up his spine as things started to fall into place. The struggle he'd had answering the question paper—the words he'd known but not been able to find. The tiredness. The loss of motor control in his right hand. The paper he'd been going to use for his assignment, that he'd not been able to understand. And adrenaline. How could he not have remembered adrenaline for anaphylaxis? He *knew* that!

'No. Don't call her. She's busy with the kids.' Hell, he couldn't even manage a simple opposites test without pausing to think, and the finger of fear turned into an icy hand clutching at his throat. 'Um—I need to see the family of that woman.'

'No, you don't. Someone else can do it. Stay here. I'll get someone to take you down to CT.'

'No! I can—' What? What could he do? Nothing, it seemed. He was so, so tired, but he got up anyway, and walked down to the scanner under his own steam. He wasn't being pushed through his own hospital on a stretcher. Lucy would know about it before he was even in the scanner, but it seemed a hell of a long way there and he could have sworn it had moved.

He sagged back against the pillows and gave in as a fleet of people appeared and took over in the scanner room.

They gave him an injection of contrast medium, and he felt it flash through his body in a hot wave as they slid him inside the body of the scanner.

'Keep nice and still and just breathe normally. That's great.'

It seemed like for ever, but it was only a few minutes before he was called into Raj's office. 'We've got the results.'

'And?' he said, his voice edgy.

Raj frowned, and he knew instantly he wasn't going to like what was coming. 'Not good news, I'm afraid. There's a mass over the left side of your frontal lobe.'

He turned the screen so Andy could see it, and as he stared at it he felt the blood drain from his head, and his heart rate kicked up as the adrenaline began to surge through his body. It looked huge, menacing.

Life threatening?

He hauled in a breath. 'What kind of mass is it? Come on, Raj, I'm a doctor, give it to me straight. Could it be a bleed?'

'No. It isn't a bleed. It could be a tumour of some sort. It's overlapping the superior temporal gyrus and Broca's area, part of your speech centre, which I think is why you're struggling to express yourself. There's some weakness on your right hand side, as well, because the motor area's right there, too. Does that make sense? Stop me if you don't understand anything. I don't want to assume you just know what I'm talking about.'

He nodded. Oh, he knew, all right. He only wished he didn't. 'No, it all makes sense.' Far too much sense. He swore, softly but succinctly, and closed his eyes. 'That's why I can't find words,' he mumbled. 'Thought I was just tired.'

'You are tired. You will be tired. You'll need an MRI scan in the morning, which will give us more information so we can decide on a course of treatment. And you'll need referring to a specialist centre.'

'What if it isn't treatable?'

Raj frowned again. 'We'll cross that bridge if we get to it. Until we know what kind of mass it is exactly, I don't want to speculate, but it'll need a biopsy for accurate diagnosis.'

He felt his muscles tighten in a flight response. For two pins he'd get up and run away, but that was ridiculous. He was a doctor. He knew about this stuff. He could deal with it. He breathed in and out slowly, and then nodded again.

'OK,' he said, and forced himself to stay there and listen to what Raj was saying.

'This has obviously been growing for some time. You say you've had symptoms for a while?'

'Mmm. We've got a new baby. Seven months—nearly eight. She's still not going through the night properly. And I've been doing a course. Lot of work. I've just done the terminal exam.' God, he was tired, and talking was so hard. The words were just sliding away. 'Thought I was just tired because of everything, but obviously not.'

'OK. Why don't you have a rest now? We'll take you up to Neurology and settle you in a side room while we run a few more tests, and I'll come and talk to you again soon.'

'No. Can't we do this quietly?' he asked, feeling a sudden rush of desperation. 'I don't want Lucy knowing. Not until we know more. I don't really need to go to the ward, do I?'

Raj frowned. 'Not really, not if you don't want to. I can

do the tests here. I don't need to keep you in tonight if you'd rather I didn't, but I'll take the bloods today so we can get started, and we'll do the scan first thing tomorrow and take more of a history, and go from there. You can go home as soon as I've got the bloods, if you want.'

'I do want.'

It would be easier, he thought as Raj quickly filled several tubes with blood, if he had a home to go to where he was welcome, but he didn't, not if Lucy had anything to say about it, he thought with bitterness and a shiver of apprehension. Then the practicalities hit him. His car was here, in the hospital car park, and even though he knew what the answer would be, still he asked the question.

'Can I drive?'

Raj shook his head, and Andy felt his life ebbing away from him.

'I'm sorry. Not for a while. Press that with your finger. And you can't work, either. I'm signing you off sick until further notice.'

He stared at the plaster Raj stuck over the needle site. Further notice? How long was that, for heaven's sake?

A month? A year?

For ever?

It was six thirty, over five hours since Raj had yanked him off the emergency department and into an alien universe.

He walked into the ED, went to his office and phoned James, the clinic lead, and told him the news.

'Don't spread it around. I don't want the details of this out. Just tell everyone I'm off sick. Tell them it's stress. Tell them whatever lie you like, I don't care. Just—don't tell them that.'

'OK. Andy—if there's anything I can do...'

'Yeah. Thanks.'

He hung up and left the building, wondering when—if—he'd ever come back in here again in an official capacity.

'Are you all right, Mr Gallagher?'

He gave the receptionist a fleeting smile. 'Yes, Jane, I'm fine, thank you, or I will be after a few days' rest.'

Lies again, but he wasn't telling her what he wasn't telling his own wife yet. He contemplated getting her to call him a cab, but he was still reeling from the news and it was just as easy to walk home, and the fresh air might clear his head.

He gave a grunt of laughter. Fat chance. It would take more than a bit of fresh air to clear this monster out of his head.

He collected a few things from the car, eyed it with regret and walked home in the tail end of the wind which had killed Jean Darby and her husband earlier today. He thought of her distress as she was asking about him, her rings, the years of love they represented, all gone in an instant.

At least he was still alive, and, if it came to that, he'd have time to say goodbye...

It was almost seven by the time he got home, and he walked into a scene of domestic chaos, welcomed by the dog and the children, but not by Lucy who was swiping at Lottie's face and hands with a baby wipe.

'I thought you were coming at three. We've been expecting you,' she said reproachfully.

Because he'd promised, he thought, and felt sick. 'Sorry. I got held up,' he said, truthfully if a little economically, and she gave a soft snort and turned away. He sucked in a breath and turned to his children, dredging up a smile.

'So, kids, did you have a good time with Grannie and Grandpa this week?'

'Yes, it was brilliant,' Emily said, her eyes sparkling.

'We went to the zoo, and I touched an elephant's trunk and it was all rough and hairy and scratchy, and the end was sticky and disgusting. It was awesome.'

He laughed, a hollow, rather desperate sound, and then listened to Megan talking about the monkeys, and then Em had a story about the meerkats, and they would have been there all evening if Lucy hadn't cut it short.

'Bedtime, girls. You need to go upstairs and put your dirty clothes in the bin while I bath Lottie, then you can have a bath and get to bed. You've had quite enough excitement this week and it's a school day tomorrow.'

'Daddy, will you read to us?' Megan asked, her eyes so like Lucy's pleading with him.

'Yes, darling. Of course I will.'

'Can I choose our story?' she asked, but then Em chipped in and they started arguing about which story they wanted.

'I'll read them both. And I'll read one to Lottie. In fact,' he said, ignoring Lucy's glare, 'why don't I go and bath her while you two put all the toys away?'

And lifting his sticky little daughter out of the high chair, he carried her upstairs and into the bathroom, still slightly numb inside. 'You're a mess, little one,' he said, turning on the taps and stripping her of the food-magnet clothes and trying not to speculate on whether he'd see her grow up. See her walk. Hear her call him Daddy...

He checked the mat in the bottom of the bath to make sure the temperature indicator hadn't changed colour, then checked it with his hand, and finally lowered her into it.

'What a little grub you are!' he said lovingly, the numbness thawing to leave an agonising ache in its place. 'Where's that sponge?'

He cleaned her face tenderly, washed the food out of her hair and blew a raspberry on her tummy, making her giggle.

She grabbed his face, scrunching his cheeks up with her fingers, her sharp little nails gouging into his skin. 'Ouch, little monkey. That hurts,' he said, and he gently prised her fingers off and straightened up, chuckling as she giggled again and made another swipe for his nose.

'Why *are* you so late, Andy?'

The soft voice behind him almost made him jump. It shouldn't have done. He'd known she'd come up the moment she could, to challenge him.

'I told you, I was held up.'

'But it's too late. They've been waiting for you since three. Why couldn't you be here then? Why can you never, ever do what you say you're going to?'

He gritted his teeth, unwilling to tell her the truth, at least until he had some answers. 'I got held up,' he repeated. 'I told you that. And I know it's late, but they're still up, and like I said, I wanted to spend some time with them.'

'You should have been here earlier. They've got school tomorrow, and you'll only get them overexcited and they won't sleep properly, and it's my first day at work tomorrow, you know that. I wanted a quiet evening to prepare.'

'So go and prepare. I'm not stopping you. Far from it. And I've moved back in, by the way.'

'No.'

'Yes,' he said, equally firmly. 'I'm not a cat, Lucy. I've told you that before. You can't just put me out of the door when it suits you. This is my home, too.'

'Not in front of the children,' she murmured warningly, and turned to hug Megan who'd run up to her.

'We've put all the toys away. Can Daddy bath us, too?'

'I expect so. He seems to be Superman tonight.'

And with that she walked off, leaving him with Megan hanging over the edge of the bath and splashing a giggling

Lottie, while he fought back the stinging in his eyes and wondered when and how it had all gone so horribly wrong.

"'And they all lived happily ever after.'"

Why did they all end like that? It cut through him like a knife, slashing him with the uncertainty of his future, the exact diagnosis lurking just out of reach, the fear of the unknown gnawing at his insides and racking him with grief.

'More!' Emily said, but Megan's eyes were drooping, and he knew Emily would soon fall asleep.

'No,' he said, although in truth he could have carried on all night, under the circumstances, cuddled up with his precious little daughters. 'Come on. Snuggle down, Megan. Emily, back in your own bed, darling. Time for sleep now. You've got school tomorrow.'

He shut the book and put it down on the pile, tucked them in and kissed them both goodnight, then turned off the light and pulled the bedroom door to, leaving just a chink of light to chase away the monsters.

Lottie was fast asleep long ago, lying flat on her back, little arms thrown up above her head, her rosebud lips slightly parted. She reminded him so much of Emily at the same age.

He closed her door again, leaving the same little chink of light, and went into the bedroom that until now he'd shared with Lucy. She was sitting on the bed, stony faced, waiting for him.

'Have you been here all week?'

'There didn't seem to be any point in staying in the hotel when you weren't even here to object,' he pointed out.

'But we're back now, so are you going to explain why you think you're staying here tonight? Why you've just moved back in without asking me? I thought we were going to discuss this?'

'We are—and I don't *think* I'm staying here, I *am* stay-ing here, and I don't have to explain to you,' he said stub-bornly, because tonight, of all nights, explaining was the last thing he wanted to do. 'I have every right to be here. Anyway, don't worry, you won't have to share a bed with me. I can sleep in the attic.'

'Good,' she said, dashing a hope he hadn't even realised he was harbouring, and he swallowed hard and opened his side of the wardrobe, pulling out clean clothes for the morning.

'If you're hungry, you'll have to go and forage in the kitchen. You were so late I just assumed you weren't com-ing, so I haven't got anything cooked for you.'

'I'm not hungry,' he said truthfully. 'I've eaten.' Sand-wiches from the staff canteen at lunchtime and a couple of biscuits with a cup of tea in Raj's office, but he wasn't telling her that.

He could feel her eyes boring into him, hear her mind working.

'I thought the idea was you'd get your exam out of the way and then we'd talk. Strikes me there's not been a lot of talking, so how come you think it's all right to move back?'

'I need to be here. There are things I need in the study, stuff I want to sort out,' he said, again truthfully, even if it was only part of the truth this time. 'And I want to spend time with the girls. Read to them.' Like tonight, maybe for the last time. 'I thought that was what you wanted?'

'Is that why you just read them five stories?'

Had he? Probably. Five hundred wouldn't have been enough.

'Guilt's an ugly thing,' she went on. 'You can't make it all up to them on one night, you know. It needs a concerted effort, change of lifestyle. And so far you aren't doing so great, are you?'

He closed his eyes and counted to ten. 'I'm well aware of that,' he said, his teeth gritted. 'I'm going to put this stuff upstairs, and then I'm going in the study. You don't need to bother about me. I'll be out first thing in the morning, you won't even see me.'

'Where's your car? How did you get home?'

'I walked. It's at the hospital. The service light came on. The garage are going to pick it up tomorrow.'

Lies again. This was the first time he'd lied to her. The first out-and-out lies, at least, in all their marriage, and now he was doing it all the time. He'd tell her the truth tomorrow, but for tonight he'd just wanted to spend time with the girls without having to deal with Lucy's emotions. It was hard enough dealing with his own, and now he just wanted to be alone so he didn't have to pretend any more. And he certainly didn't want to start talking about their future, not when he didn't even know if he had one.

Scooping up his things, he walked out of their bedroom, flicked on the upper landing light and walked firmly up the stairs. He wasn't going to weaken. He wasn't going to go downstairs and sit with her, and pour his heart out.

Anything could happen. Until he'd had a biopsy there was no knowing what they'd find. It might be easily treatable, or it might be highly aggressive. And then where would Lucy be?

No. If she was angry with him, if she was ready to make a break from him, then he'd let her, for her sake and the children's. It would be so much easier for them that way. And anyway, a large part of him was still angry with her for issuing that ultimatum two weeks ago. If she could do that, if she was prepared to throw it all away without giving him a chance, then maybe it really *was* over.

So he put his things in the larger attic bedroom, went downstairs to make himself a drink and a sandwich and shut himself away in the study. He had things to check—wills, details of his pension and bank accounts, life assurance, mortgage—all sorts of things needed to be looked at, put together, so if the worse came to the worst, Lucy wouldn't have a nightmare to deal with. And it had to be done while he was still able to do it.

Ignoring the flicker of dread, he pulled open the drawer at the bottom of the bookshelves and pulled out the file.

It was all in order. He'd known it was, but he'd had to check. When, like Jean and Dennis Darby, his parents had died together in an accident, their affairs had been in chaos. It had taken him ages to sort it all out, and he'd vowed that his family would never have to deal with the mess he'd been left with.

It was typical of them, though. He'd loved them dearly, but they'd never made a plan and stuck to it in their lives. His schooling had been constantly disrupted by their moves from one opportunity to another, and he'd grown used to making new friends and working hard to catch up in every new school. He'd done it because he'd had no choice, but he hadn't enjoyed it, unlike his parents who thrived on every challenge life threw at them.

It hadn't all been bad, he remembered fondly. His childhood had been filled with love and laughter, but it had also been riddled with upheaval and financial uncertainty, and he'd vowed his own children wouldn't have to put up with the same chaotic lifestyle, and they certainly wouldn't find his affairs in total disarray if anything happened to him.

But there was no mess. He'd already taken care of that, and if the worse came to the worst...

The flicker of fear made his chest tighten, but he ignored it. He wasn't going to dwell on the dark side of this. Not until and unless he had to. He made another drink and carried his laptop back up with him. He'd spend the rest of the evening researching all the things that could be going on in his head, to take his mind off his disintegrating marriage to the woman he loved with all his heart.

And then tomorrow, hopefully, he'd have some answers.

She sat there on the bed, listening as he walked up and down the stairs. He spent a few minutes in the study, then eventually he went back up to the attic bedroom, closing the door with a quiet but somehow final click.

The sound made her breath hitch, and she closed her eyes and squeezed them tight shut.

Why had he come back? She was just getting her head around being here without him, and now he was back and she felt unsettled and restless and sad.

Was it just guilt about the children that had brought him back tonight? Or had he intended to try and win her round, but she'd put him off by being defensive?

She'd seen the look in his eyes when he was talking to the girls, when he'd first walked in, and he'd looked—gosh—grief stricken, for a moment? So did that mean her plan was working, that finally it had sunk in just how much he was needed by all of them? How much he hurt them every time he broke a promise?

He'd shut himself away now—keeping out of her way so as not to intrude? She didn't think so. And he wasn't really working, despite what he'd said. If he'd been working, he would have been in his study as usual.

Maybe he felt it wasn't his any more, but that was ridiculous because he was the only one who used it, by and large. Their books were stored in there, shelf after shelf of reference books and novels and autobiographies, DIY books and How-To books, all the family photograph albums from their first holiday together through to Lottie's first few months, and all their household bills and things were filed in the cupboards at the bottom, along with all the important stuff, like birth certificates and their marriage certificate and the wills.

But it was his study, always had been, and recently it had been the place he'd retreated to more and more. So why not tonight?

She went down to the kitchen and saw an open bottle of wine on the side. He must have taken a glass upstairs.

She poured herself a glass and hesitated. Should she go up to him? Talk to him again, find out what was really motivating him? Maybe he was waiting for her, hoping she'd go up to him.

Maybe that was why he'd chosen a bedroom, she thought, rather than the study, and she ran her tongue over suddenly dry lips.

She felt a fizzle inside her, a tingle of something that could have been fear or then might have been excitement. She sipped the wine, put it down and squared her shoulders. Only one way to find out, she told herself, and headed for the stairs.

Then stopped, and walked back into the kitchen.

No. She wasn't going to make it that easy for him. If he wanted to make it up to her, to them, then he could come and talk to her. He knew where she was, and she was damned if she was going to fold first. And anyway, she reminded herself, nothing had changed. He'd been four hours later tonight than he'd said he'd be.

No. Let him sweat.

Ignoring the wine, she made herself a cup of tea, went through some information from the practice, watched a little television and went to bed, to find the lingering scent of his aftershave clinging to the sheets and tormenting her dreams.

* * *

He was up and showered and dressed by the time Lottie woke, and he went down and scooped her out of her cot and cuddled her as he carried her into their bedroom.

'Someone needs you,' he said, and Lucy emerged from the bedclothes looking rumpled and warm and so beautiful he nearly weakened.

'You're dressed.'

'I've got an early appointment,' he said glibly, kissing Lottie and handing her over.

'When are you going to see the children again?'

He sucked in his breath silently. 'I don't know,' he said honestly. 'I'll give you a call.'

'OK.'

'Good luck with work today. Hope it goes well.'

'Thanks. It's only the morning. I'll be fine.'

'I'm sure you will.'

Then, because he just couldn't help himself, because she was propped up against the pillows with Lottie suckling noisily at her breast and the scene was tearing holes in his heart, he leant over and pressed his mouth to hers in a hard, brief kiss of farewell.

'Goodbye, Lucy,' he said.

And then before he could make a fool of himself and pour it all out, he walked away, glancing in on the girls just to torture himself a little more before he carried his bag downstairs. He left his laptop in the study. He wouldn't need it today. Maybe never.

He let himself out of the front door as the taxi drew up outside, and as it pulled away he glanced back and saw Lucy standing at the bedroom window. He lifted a hand, and then looked away before he crumbled and asked the driver to stop.

He had to do this—had to go to the hospital and face the future, and he had to do it alone.

CHAPTER FOUR

Raj was waiting for him in the MRI suite, and he shook his hand and then ushered him through to the changing cubicle.

'You know the form. I'm afraid you need to take everything off and put on the gown. There's a locker you can put your things in. Any metalwork we need to know about?' he asked, and Andy shook his head.

'No. All me.'

'Good. Don't forget to take off your watch and any jewellery, and come out when you're done. We're ready to go.'

No time to run away, then.

Not that he was going to, but it was ludicrously tempting.

He was taken through to the MRI scanner and lay down on the bed, his head towards the hollow tube where the scan would take place. Someone connected him up to the headphones, and left him there.

This was it, then. He'd get his answers now, thanks to this miracle machine which could see inside him with astonishing clarity. For a second, he wished it had never been invented.

'Right, lie as still as you can, but breathe normally,' a voice said through the headphones, and the scanner bed started to move.

He'd told people about them, but he'd never understood what noisy, confined things they were until he was posted into it. He hated tight spaces, always had, and his pulse rocketed.

He fought the fear, crushed it down as the thing whirred and clonked for what seemed like an age, and then at last it was over and they slid him out and Raj came and stood beside him.

'OK?'

'I'll live,' he said, and wondered if that was actually true. 'Can I see it?'

'Sure. Get your clothes on and we'll go up to my office.'

Five minutes later Raj sat him down as they scrolled through the images.

Shocking images, of the mass inside his head.

They weren't meaningless to him, of course, and certainly not meaningless in terms of their possible implications, but he knew Raj could understand far more from these slices of his brain than he ever would.

'I can't give you any definite answers,' he said quietly. 'I'm sorry, the only way is a biopsy, and I need to refer you for that. This is going to take specialist equipment we simply don't have, and I want to fast-track you. I won't beat about the bush, this is big, and I think you're deteriorating fast now. Do you have any preference for neurosurgeons?'

He felt a wave of nausea and crushed it. 'Yes. David Cardew. I trained with him, and I still see him quite often at conferences and things. I think he's got a good reputation.'

Raj nodded. 'He is good. Do you want to give him a call, or shall I?'

'I'd better break the news first. Will you talk to him then?'

'Sure.'

He called his old college friend, and got his voicemail, so he rang the hospital and was put through to his secretary.

'I'll get him to call you straight away,' she promised, and two minutes later his mobile rang.

'Andy, hi, how're you doing?'

'Not great,' he said without preamble. 'David, I've got a problem. A mass on the left side of my temporal lobe. It's over Broca's, and it's not small.'

David swore softly. 'Got the scans? Who's your consultant?'

'Rajiv Patel. He wants to fast-track me. He's right here with me—want to talk to him?'

'If I could.'

He handed the phone over, and sat there listening to a one-sided conversation that he'd rather not have heard. There was the truth, after all, and then the whole truth.

Frankly, he could have done with a bunch of lies.

'He wants to talk to you again.'

He took the phone back. 'Get everything you need?'

'Yeah. Give me a few minutes to look at these—Raj is sending them over now. I'll call you, but from what he says, you need a biopsy. I've got a slot tomorrow, if that helps.'

'Tomorrow?'

'I can't do it today, much as I'd like to.'

He laughed. 'I didn't expect you to. I was thinking, maybe, a week or so.'

'No. Let me look at the images, and I'll come right back to you.'

He slid the phone back into his pocket and met Raj's eyes. 'So—he says he could do the biopsy tomorrow.'

'Yes. I'm sorry, Andy. I wish I could have told you something better, but I can't. You'll be in good hands, though.'

'Yeah. Thanks, Raj. I'll let you know what he says.'

He got himself a coffee from the café and went and sat in his car outside, for want of anywhere more private to wait, and while he was there he called the garage and asked them to collect the car and service it. He couldn't just leave it at the hospital indefinitely and at least they could return it to his home.

'Well, I think it's a meningioma, arising from the arachnoid membrane surrounding the brain, rather than a tumour in the cerebral cortex itself,' David said when he called back a short while later.

'That's good news, isn't it?' he asked, checking before he allowed himself to feel relieved.

'Very good news. If you're going to have a brain tumour, it's the one to have. That said, it's pretty extensive. It's right over Broca's area, which seems to control the way we express words rather than understand them. I understand from Raj you've got a slight speech loss—expressive aphasia, so you can understand everything but not speak as fluently, and it's also affecting the motor control of your right side, especially your hand, but that you can understand everything that's said. Does that make sense to you, fit your symptoms?'

'Yes. Mostly I'm fine. It's only complicated stuff, really, or odd things that I'm having trouble with. And my right hand's been shaking for a while, off and on. I thought it was just stress and tiredness. It's all much worse when I'm tired.'

'Yes. It would be, because you're compensating with all the day-to-day things, and it's only the really high-level stuff that you've lost at this stage. So—surgery. I'm pretty sure I'm right about it being a meningioma, so I think we'll bypass the biopsy and just cut to the chase. I'd like to operate tomorrow, if that's all right with you?'

'Tomorrow?' he echoed, shocked. 'I thought you'd only have time to do a biopsy?'

'No. I had a long elective procedure booked, but the patient's had to cancel, he's got flu. So I have a long enough slot. Otherwise we might be talking a couple of weeks and from what Raj has said, I don't want to leave you any longer than I have to. Can you get down here today so we can run a few more tests and take a thorough history?'

'Um—sure. Where's the clinic?'

'I'll email you the link. It's easy to find. And don't worry about it, Andy. We'll get you sorted. This is the kind of stuff I deal with every day.'

Was it? He was glad he was sitting down, because he felt the blood leave his head and a wave of nausea swept over him. It suddenly all seemed incredibly real. 'Um— how are you intending to do it?'

'Awake craniotomy. It's too large for an endoscopic technique, and I need access to the margins to make sure I've got it all. And I need you awake because of the speech implications. We'll need to map the language areas.'

Under normal circumstances he would have found the idea fascinating. Not today. 'Can you tell from the scans if it's benign or malignant?'

'Not without a biopsy which we'll do at the same time, but it hasn't invaded the cerebral cortex or the dura as far as I can tell from the scans, so that's a positive sign. However, it does look as if it's following some of the tight fissures in Broca's area. And that has implications for the prognosis.'

He didn't like the sound of that. 'Permanent implications?' he asked warily.

'I hope not. It could, however, be significant post-op. You might find you lose your speech totally or almost totally for a while until the swelling and bruising caused by the surgery has healed and your brain's recovered from the sustained pressure of the tumour. That's why I want to do it as soon as possible.'

'How long's a while?' he asked, wondering if he'd ever

practise medicine again. Not if he couldn't speak fluently, couldn't pull important information out and share it, that was for sure.

'Days. Weeks. Months, possibly, for the really high-level stuff to come back.'

'So I'll be off work for a long time?'

'Maybe. I'm hoping it won't be too long. Maybe a couple of months.'

'But that's assuming it's not malignant and it hasn't migrated into the brain tissue?'

'Andy, this is all speculation. I can't tell you any more until I've operated on you tomorrow. And I really need to do it while you're awake. Are you OK with that?'

Was he? He sucked in a long, slow breath, and nodded. It was the best way. He'd seen documentaries about it but now it had a new relevance, so last night he'd been reading up on it, watching video clips on the internet, and knew that they used electrodes to identify parts of the brain used for specific functions, so they knew which parts were important for which tasks. And for that mapping process, he'd have to be awake and responsive.

He swallowed. 'Yes. I'm fine with it.'

And then he thought about Lucy, and shut his eyes.

'I should tell my wife.'

'You still haven't told her?'

'No. I wanted to know more.' And now he did, there was no excuse for delaying.

'Do you want me to talk to her?'

'No. I'll tell her. It'll be better coming from me.'

But she rejected his call. She was probably still at work, he told himself, but even so, he needed her, needed that contact desperately, and as he walked home to pack his bags, he felt more isolated than he'd ever felt in his life.

* * *

She didn't answer the phone.

She was in a café with Daisy Walker, with Lottie and Daisy's Thomas in high chairs making a mess with biscuits, and they were talking about nothing in particular while her heart was quietly breaking. She'd watched him go this morning, seen him wave, and it had seemed so—so *final*, really. She'd really hoped, now the exam was out of the way, that finally they'd talk and find a way to bridge this gulf between them, but he hadn't shown any sign of wanting to talk to her last night, and she'd hardly been able to concentrate all morning at work.

She was glad she'd arranged to meet Daisy for coffee after she'd finished her surgery. Anything rather than sitting at home and wallowing in self-pity for the rest of the day.

And when the phone rang, she hesitated, just in case it was him, but she couldn't ignore it. It might be the school.

It wasn't. It was Andy.

She hesitated, then rejected the call. She didn't want to talk to him now. She'd call him back later, when she was alone. But not yet.

'How about another coffee?' she asked Daisy brightly. 'I can't be bothered to go home and tackle the washing.'

'Nor can I. I'll get them. What was yours? Skinny decaf cappuccino?'

'Please.'

But then it ran again, while Daisy was still rummaging in her bag for her purse, and she answered it this time.

'Andy, I'm a bit busy at the moment, I'm having coffee with Daisy. Will it keep?'

'Not really. I need to talk to you pretty urgently.'

'I only saw you this morning. How can it be that urgent?' she asked, impatient with him because everything—

everything—always had to be done to suit him, and she'd spent the whole morning in knots.

'D'you know what? Forget it,' he said crisply, and hung up.

And then Daisy's phone rang. 'Sorry, I need to take this, it's Ben,' she said, and she answered it, then looked across at Lucy and frowned thoughtfully. 'I don't know. No, she hasn't mentioned it and she's just spoken to him. Yes, I'll ask her. OK, darling. Thank you.'

She sat down again. 'Lucy, that was Ben,' she said softly. 'He said to ask you how Andy is.'

'Andy? I don't know. He was fine this morning when he went to work. Why?'

'Because he didn't go to work today. He's off sick, apparently, and Ben saw him coming out of Raj Patel's office. And yesterday he had a CT scan.'

'What?'

Her blood ran cold. Raj was a neurologist. And he'd had a CT scan? Why hadn't he told her last night? Was that what he'd been phoning to tell her just now? And she'd all but told him to go to hell...

'Lucy?' Daisy took Lucy's hands in hers, her face concerned. 'Talk to me.'

'He just rang me,' she said, her voice sounding hollow and far away. 'He said it was urgent, and I told him I was busy. Daisy, I've got to go to him. I had no idea there was anything wrong...'

She broke off, sucking in a breath, trying to keep calm.

'What can I do?' Daisy asked, quietly and calmly taking command of the situation.

Oh, help, the children. 'Could you have Lottie? Just for now. I don't even know where he is.'

'Ring him.'

She rang, and eventually he picked up. She didn't even let him speak, just pitched in, distraught.

'Andy, where are you? Are you at the hospital still? Why didn't you tell me you were sick?'

She heard a quiet sigh. 'I tried, Lucy,' he pointed out, and she felt the guilt spiral. 'I'm at home, but not for long. I've got to go to London.'

'Not without me. Whatever it is, you're not going without me. I'm coming home now. Don't you dare leave without me.'

She scrambled to her feet, gathering up her things, her heart racing. 'Daisy, we have to go to London—'

'Go home. I'll take Thomas home and come round in the car to pick Lottie up. I'll look after her, and the dog, and I'll get the girls after school. You don't have to worry about a thing. Go—shoo.'

She went, hurrying along the pavements with the buggy, dodging pedestrians and feeling choked with fear, and then he was opening the door and she fell into his arms.

'I'm so sorry—'

'Shh. Don't upset Lottie. Just help me pack.'

'Can I come? I know I've been a complete bitch to you, but please let me come, whatever it is.'

'Of course you can come. And you haven't been any worse than me, but I can't do this now, Lucy. I know things are a mess. I just—not now, OK?'

The doorbell rang, and she snatched it open and let Daisy in. 'Daisy's going to have the children.'

'Bless you,' Andy said, and hugged her. 'Thanks.'

'I'll get some stuff.' She ran upstairs on legs of rubber, threw things for all the girls into a bag and handed it to Daisy, then kissed Lottie goodbye and put her into the car seat that Andy must have moved. 'I'll call my parents—

they'll come and get them from you. Here, give them my keys. Thank you so, so much.'

'No problem. Come on, Stanley. In the car.'

She loaded the dog into the boot with the bag of clothes, and as she pulled off the drive Andy headed for the stairs.

'I need to pack,' he said, and went up, leaving her to follow. There was so much he wanted to tell her, so much he needed to say, but there was a gulf between them that not even this could bridge adequately.

'Talk to me,' she pleaded. Her eyes were wide with fear and shock, and he could feel her shaking all over. 'Andy? What's going on?'

'I've got a brain tumour,' he said, curiously detached.

'A brain tumour?'

He nodded. 'David Cardew thinks it's a meningioma,' he said, and she went chalk white and sat down suddenly on the bed, her fingers threaded through his and locked on tight. He gripped back, curiously relieved that she'd come home to him. Not that it changed anything, but—

'How did you find out? What made you think there was anything wrong?'

'Raj spotted it yesterday. He came to the ED, and he noticed I was stumbling over my words, and he did a CT—'

'Why didn't you say anything? Last night—you came home, and you didn't say anything! Why ever not?'

'I just—I wanted it to be normal,' he said, and she could see his jaw working. 'I wanted—'

He couldn't go on, so she finished the sentence for him, her heart breaking.

'You wanted to read to the girls,' she whispered, and he nodded.

'Raj fast-tracked me to David Cardew, and he says after the op I might lose my speech for a while.'

She closed her eyes, the implications only just sinking

in. 'Where is it?' she asked, dreading the answer. 'This tumour?'

'On the side of my left frontal lobe. Over Broca's.'

She flinched, the significance not lost on her. 'Does he think he can get it out?'

'I think so. He's going to operate tomorrow morning. That's part of the hurry. It's causing the aphasia.'

The aphasia she hadn't even noticed, but come to think of it, he'd been less communicative, less talkative and certainly not himself. 'Expressive aphasia.'

'Yeah. I can understand everything—well, not everything. I read a research paper the other day and couldn't understand it, but that could have been because it was pretentious crap. It's finding words. It's driving me nuts. I can't—I know exactly what I'm trying to say, it's all there, I just can't find the exact words. Most of the time it's fine, I can wing it, but difficult stuff—it's just not there, and some of the easy stuff is getting harder. And it's getting rapidly worse.' He hesitated, then went on, 'I thought I was just tired, but my hand's been funny, as well. Shaking. Weaker. I've been ignoring it—in denial, I suppose, but it's because the tumour's over the motor control area for my right side, as well as Broca's, so it's having a motor effect, as well.'

Which was why his handwriting was untidy. So many clues, and she'd missed them all. Lucy felt sick. Sick with fear, sick with guilt, sick with worry.

'I'm so sorry—'

'No. Not now, Luce. I can't do this now. I know our marriage is a mess, and this doesn't change it, and it'll probably be worse afterwards, but I can't deal with that now. I just need to get through this.'

She nodded numbly. 'OK. Can I stay with you? I know

I kicked you out, but it wasn't because I don't care. I do care. I care a lot—so much. Please let me stay with you.'

His fingers tightened, and he nodded. 'Course you can,' he said gruffly.

He wrapped his arms around her and held her tight, and she clung to him, her body shaking all over with reaction. He could feel her crying, feel the sobs breaking free, and he lifted her face and kissed away the tears.

'Don't cry.'

'I can't help it,' she said brokenly. 'I can't lose you.'

'Don't—you won't lose me. I'm here.'

She touched his cheek, her fingers trembling. 'I love you.'

He gave a ragged groan and gave up. He needed her, as he'd never needed her, and he bent his head and took her mouth in a long, frenzied kiss, his fingers tunnelling through her hair, his hands all over her, searching for her skin, dragging the soft sweater out of the way and sliding his hands around her ribcage.

So soft. So sweet. God, he'd missed her. And if the operation went wrong...

She was tugging at his shirt, but there wasn't time for that and he hauled up her skirt, unzipped his trousers and pushed her back onto the bed, driving into her with a desperate groan.

It wasn't subtle. It was frantic and messy and fraught with emotion, and the end when it came left him reeling.

He dropped his head on her shoulder and sucked in a breath, and her hands gentled, stroking his shoulders, sliding down his back and soothing him tenderly.

'I love you,' she murmured, and he lifted his head and stared down into her tear-filled eyes, and felt his own flood.

'Lucy, this doesn't change things. I don't want you feeling you're stuck with me because of this. If the surgery doesn't work out—'

'Shh.' She pressed her finger to his lips and eased away from him. 'Come on, we have to pack. We've got a train to catch.'

'Mr Gallagher? Mr Cardew will see you now.'

He stood up. 'Coming?'

She nodded and got to her feet, and went in with him, her legs like jelly.

David greeted them warmly, but then dispensed with the pleasantries and got straight to the point.

'I'm sorry about the unseemly rush, but you probably don't mind. Right, this is what we're dealing with.'

She looked at the images on the screen in front of them, and she felt Andy's fingers thread through hers again and tighten. She squeezed back, and kept his hand firmly in hers while David talked to them.

He told them exactly what he planned to do, and she was shocked by the extent of the pale shape sprawled across the left side of his frontal lobe.

All the way there she'd convinced herself it could only be tiny, just a trivial little blip pressing on his brain, but there was nothing slight or trivial about it, she realised in dread, and the fallout from the surgery could be huge. And that was assuming that it was benign.

The significance of it wasn't lost on Andy, either, she realised, because as David started explaining in detail what he intended to do, his fingers tightened on hers again and she could feel the tension vibrating through him.

She felt overwhelmed, staring at the extensive mass that David was planning on slowly and painstakingly dissecting out. It followed every line and contour of his speech area, snuggling down into every nook and cranny. Getting it out will be a nightmare, she thought. What if he loses his speech completely? What if he can't ever talk to me again? Or the children?

She thought of his dry wit, the hilarious stories he told at dinner parties, his effortless eloquence. He had an opinion on just about everything, and expressed himself so fluently, so clearly, so lucidly. If he couldn't do that, couldn't even manage the normal everyday communication of essentials, the frustration would kill him, even if the tumour didn't.

'I want to operate first thing tomorrow morning,' David was saying. 'We've discussed this briefly, but I'll go over it again. We'll give you all kinds of lovely happy drugs, take you into Theatre and give you a brief anaesthetic while we remove the area of skull over the tumour, and then we wake you up. If you can tolerate it, and it should be pain free, we'll take a biopsy of the tumour and get it sent off, and then we'll ask you to talk to us and read out loud until we've established what part of the affected area is controlling what, and then we'll know what we can and can't achieve. If you get speech arrest at any point in the procedure, we'll have to assess where to go from there.'

He'd be in Theatre for ages, she thought numbly. Awake, and lying there trying to concentrate while they carefully nibbled away at this insidious thing inside the head of the man she loved.

'How long will it take?' she asked, knowing it could only be a guess but struggling for any kind of common sense from this.

'A few hours. Four, maybe, at the most? We'll keep you in overnight tonight, Andy, and run some more tests before the morning. I've got a speech and language therapist coming to do a pre-op assessment, and she'll repeat that tomorrow after the procedure and then she'll be working with your local SLT as necessary in the next few weeks or months. You're welcome to stay here, Lucy; there's a reclining chair and some blankets in the room, and we'll keep updating you with progress tomorrow as we go.'

'How long will I be in?' Andy asked, his voice sounding rusty and unused.

'It depends how you are. Probably one night post-op. Maybe not even that. Once you're stable and I'm satisfied there are no post-op complications, you can go home. I'll get them to show you to your room now and they can start to clerk you.'

It was a lovely room, a single room off the quiet ward overlooking a tree-lined courtyard, and Lucy perched on the edge of the reclining chair while Andy paced restlessly.

'What about the children?' he asked, worrying about them, about the fact that he hadn't been able to see them and explain—might never be able to explain. 'Will your parents be all right to have them that long?'

'They'll be fine. They're going to stay at ours. Daisy's got my keys. I'll call them later, and we'll update them again tomorrow. After the op. When I know—' She broke off. When she knew he was alive? When she knew he wouldn't die? *When she knew that he'd never talk again?*

Damn, she was crying, and while she mopped herself up Andy just stood there staring numbly out of the window.

'Sorry,' she said, sniffing. 'It's just such a shock.'

He nodded. 'I know.'

He looked as if he was going to say more, but then there was a knock on the door and a smiling woman came in armed with a folder.

'Hi, are you Andrew Gallagher?'

'Yes. Andy. And this is my wife, Lucy.'

'Hi, there. I'm Kate North, I'm the speech and language therapist. Is it OK if I call you Andy and Lucy?'

'Sure.'

'Right, I don't know how much you know about this. A fair amount, I imagine? I gather you're both doctors?'

'Yes, that's right,' Lucy said, warming to her. 'So—what happens now?'

'I'd like to do a test to establish where you are at the moment with your speech, Andy. Is that OK?'

'That's fine. Go ahead.'

'Do you want me to leave?' Lucy asked him, wondering he'd want her there or if he'd feel less uncomfortable without her.

He shrugged, but Kate gave her an encouraging smile. 'I'm fine with you staying. You're the person he talks to most, so it's actually quite useful for you to know what we do and how we establish speech loss, and you can give me an idea of what you would have expected him to be capable of.'

She nodded. 'I would be interested,' she admitted. 'I'm a GP, so I have lots of stroke patients I refer for SLT. It would be very useful to see it in action.'

'Sure. Right, let's start.'

It was simple. Dead easy, he thought, having no trouble at all with any of the exercises. Then they shifted up a gear, and he had the odd hesitation, but Kate didn't seem fazed by it and moved on.

And he began to struggle. Really struggle, with things he *knew*. And it shook him.

As if she realised that, she shut her folder and smiled. 'OK, I think we've done enough now. I'll be able to tell after the op just how much of an effect, if any, it's had on you, and I'll pass that onto the SLT you'll be working with at home in Suffolk so she knows where to start.'

He nodded, and with a reassuring smile and a handshake, she left them again.

'Wow. That was quite intensive,' Lucy said, but he didn't reply. He was still busy taking in the shocking extent of the holes in his expressive language ability that her tests had revealed, an extent he'd been blissfully unaware of except for the odd moment of frustration.

No. More than that, if he was honest, but nothing that couldn't have been put down to distraction or tiredness. But the tests she'd just done proved to him beyond any doubt that this was serious and significant.

And in that moment, it went from theory to reality.

There were other tests.

Swabs for MRSA, even though they'd been done in Yoxburgh on Sunday. Bloods, ditto. A full physical examination from the anaesthetist, and another talk-through of the procedure, as if he wasn't well enough aware of what they were going to do to him.

In a gap in the middle he spoke to the children, assured them that he was all right, told them he loved them and then handed the phone to Lucy because his throat closed up so he couldn't speak.

'Are they OK?' he asked when she hung up, and she nodded.

'I think so. They've had supper and they're about to get ready for bed. My parents send their love, and Daisy and Ben said break a leg, apparently. Oh, and Stanley's dug a hole in the lawn.'

He gave a tiny, twisted smile, and then another nurse came in for another set of obs and the merry-go-round started all over again.

And then finally, at seven o'clock, they were left alone.

'So what happens now?' he asked a nurse who popped in to check his notes.

'Supper. You have a choice—there's a menu here, or if

you'd rather you can go out for dinner. There's a nice Italian place round the corner.'

'Can we do that?' he asked, sounding stunned.

'Yes, sure. Just don't have anything too heavy, and don't drink too much.'

'One glass of wine?'

She smiled. 'One glass of wine is fine. Go out of the door, turn right and right again, and it's in the mews, about half way down on the left. Be back by nine, if you can.'

She walked out, and Andy let out a tiny, amazed huff of laughter and looked at Lucy. 'Well, are you coming?'

'Absolutely.'

She stood up and pulled on her jacket, and Andy shrugged into his coat and opened the door for her, looking as if he'd been reprieved.

He held out his arm, and she tucked her hand into the crook of it and they walked out together into the chilly November night, arm in arm, for all the world like any other married couple.

If only...

CHAPTER FIVE

THEY found the restaurant easily, and because it was Monday night and quite early, there was a table free.

'So, what do you fancy?' he asked, scanning the menu.

'Nothing, really. It's just nice to get out of the hospital.'

He put the menu down and smiled at her, his slate blue eyes curiously intense. 'Forget it, Lucy. Let's forget everything for the next couple of hours. Just you and me, a nice meal, a glass of wine.'

Because it might be the last conversation they ever had.

She held his eyes for an age, spellbound by that strange intensity, and then nodded and looked down at her menu. 'OK. I'll have the crayfish arrabiatta, and then probably tiramisu. And a glass of prosecco, I think.'

'Sounds good to me.'

He hailed the waiter, placed the order and then took her hand, his eyes gentle now, warm and tender. 'Thanks for coming with me.'

She swallowed. 'I wouldn't have let you come on your own. I've missed you. It's felt—wrong.'

He ignored that. 'Tell me about work. How did it feel going back?'

'OK, I suppose. I was a bit worried about Lottie at nursery, but she was fine.' And you, only you weren't fine, were you, she thought, but didn't say it. 'Actually, I'd better let them know I won't be in for a while.'

'Why not?'

'Because I'll be looking after you.'

'No, you won't. I'll be fine. And anyway, we weren't talking about that,' he said with a smile that didn't seem to reach quite to his eyes. 'Tell me about Ben and Daisy's house. Have you seen it yet?'

She let it go for now. Curiously liberating, she realised, and smiled back, playing along with him because really, what else could they do? And it *was* nice to sit and talk to him as if nothing so momentous was going to happen tomorrow.

'Yes. Yes, I have seen it, a couple of times, and it's lovely, but I think they're mad. I'm so, so glad we bought a modern house because we just wouldn't cope. We still haven't got round to painting it, and all we have to do is open a tin of emulsion. They've got to strip wallpaper and replaster half of it, and the kitchen's huge, but at the moment it's almost bare and they're pretty much camping in it. She was telling me what they're going to do, and it'll be really lovely when it's finished, but—wow.'

'You always said you fancied a Victorian house.'

'No. I said I love them,' she corrected, picking up an olive and chewing it thoughtfully. 'I didn't say I'd want to live in one. The flat was enough to put me off for life.'

He laughed softly. 'It was a nightmare, wasn't it? Do you remember that night of the storm, when the plaster cornice fell down in the bedroom and nearly smashed the chest of drawers?'

'I don't think I'll ever forget it! And the landlord never did fix it. We had a hole in the ceiling for a year, and every time it rained, it dripped into a bucket.'

'That was a long time ago.'

'It was, and it should have been awful, but we had fun. We used to go out for walks and house-hunt every Sunday.'

'We did. And then we found our little house.' His thumb stroked rhythmically over the back of her hand, his smile nostalgic, and she ached to hold him. Instead she fed him an olive.

'I loved that house. And it was much better than the flat.'

'Only slightly. It was in a pretty tired state, and it had a wasp's nest in the roof instead of leaks,' he reminded her.

She laughed. 'I'd forgotten that—but it was ours, so it didn't seem to matter. It had a lovely rose bed down the side of the garden, though, and that gorgeous old brick wall behind it. Beautiful. They smelt amazing, those old roses. I really missed them when we sold that house.'

'You always loved roses,' he murmured. 'You had them in your bouquet. Real ones, scented, out of your mother's garden. They were beautiful. You were beautiful. You still are.'

Her eyes filled, and she looked down, a soft wash of co-lour flooding her cheeks. It was years since she'd blushed, he realised. Years, maybe, since he'd complimented her. What a waste.

'Lucy?'

She looked up, and saw sorrow and regret in his eyes.

'Don't, Andy. Not now. It really doesn't matter.'

She took his hand in hers, tracing the lifeline with her fingertip, wondering what secrets it held for their future.

'Scusi, Signora.'

She let his hand go and sat back so the waiter could set her plate down, and the moment was gone...

'Lucy?'

She turned her head towards him, lying in the bed close by her side. 'Mmm?'

'Come here. I want to hold you.'

She sat up, the light blanket sliding off her shoulders, and searched his face in the dim light. 'We can't!' she whispered.

'Of course we can, we're married. And anyway, who's going to know?'

'They'll come in and do your obs.'

'No, they won't. Not till the morning.'

He was right, they wouldn't, and she couldn't sleep, not when all she wanted to do was hold him. And she guessed he couldn't sleep, either, which was more significant, because tomorrow was going to be a very challenging day for him.

She slipped into bed beside him and rested her head on his shoulder, and his arm curled warm and firm around her back, his hand splayed over her hip as their legs tangled together.

'That's better,' he said softly, and within minutes he was snoring quietly, his chest rising and falling evenly as he slid into sleep. She could hear his heart beating steadily under her ear, feel the shift of his ribs under her hand with every breath.

'I love you,' she whispered silently, hot tears leaking unbidden from the corners of her eyes.

She did love him.

He might not be perfect, but he was her rock, her anchor in the choppy sea of life, and she lay there holding him, the man she'd loved for so many years, surrounded by the muffled sound of the London traffic and the quiet footfalls of the nurses in the corridor outside, keeping vigil over him until the noises outside the door signalled the start of the day.

Then she slipped quietly out of his arms and stood at the

window, watching the first faint streaks of dawn lighten the sky while she waited for the curtain to rise on the next act.

He was given a pre-med, and the 'happy drugs' David had talked about, the sedative that would keep him calm throughout the procedure, and David came to see him.

'How are you?'

'Looking forward to it being over.'

'I'm sure. Lucy, have we got your mobile number so we can keep in touch?'

'Yes. But I'll probably be here for most of it. Is that all right?'

'Of course. Do whatever you want. Any more questions, either of you?'

They shook their heads, and he squeezed Andy's hand. 'See you in there. You'll be fine. I'll look after you.'

He nodded, and David went out, closing the door softly behind him and leaving them alone.

'Do you want to speak to the girls?' she asked, and he nodded again, so she rang home and he talked briefly to both of them. Lucy was sitting beside him, perched on the edge of the chair, her hands clenched together as she watched him. His eyes were bright when he handed back the phone.

'OK?'

He nodded, unable to speak, teetering on the brink of his control. He was OK, he supposed, in a way—as OK as it could be when you'd just spoken to your children for what might be the very last time. Except...

He turned to face her, his heart thumping.

'Luce, I've written something for the kids, and for you. It's upstairs in the attic bedroom, in the top drawer of the bedside table. If anything happens—'

She caught her breath, and hastily blinked away the

tears. 'Nothing's going to happen,' she said firmly, crushing his hand. 'You're going to be fine. You heard him. He's going to get it all out, and you'll be fine.'

His smile nearly broke her heart.

'Give it to them. If you need to.'

She sucked in a breath and blinked back a fresh wave of tears.

'Of course I will. But I won't need to. David won't let anything happen to you.'

But they both knew it wasn't all down to David and his skill, and as the minutes ticked by, the tension mounted and it was almost a relief when they arrived to take him to Theatre.

He rested his head back and closed his eyes, and Lucy held his hand until they kicked the brakes off the bed.

'Time to go,' they said, pausing.

'Good luck. I love you,' she said softly as she kissed him goodbye, and as they wheeled him away she didn't hear his answer. It could have been, 'I'm sorry,' but she wasn't sure.

Her heart lurched, and she pressed her hand to her mouth to hold back the cry.

Don't be sorry. Just live. Anything else we can deal with. Just—live...

It was the longest morning of her life.

He'd been taken down to Theatre at seven fifty, and despite what she'd said about waiting there, she suddenly needed to be outside, so she went to the little café on the corner near the restaurant, and bought herself a cappuccino and a biscotti to dunk in it, and phoned her mother.

'How is he?' she asked.

'Um—he's gone to Theatre a few minutes ago. Because it's a meningioma David's confident he can get all of it without causing any damage, but it's over his speech centre, Mum, and—' She broke off, struggling with tears, and her mother waited.

'Sorry. It's just all a bit much. How's Lottie? I had to express some milk this morning, and I didn't bring the breast pump so it was a bit tricky. Was she all right with the bottle?'

'She's fine. We're all fine. She woke once in the night but she settled again. She's spreading her breakfast in her hair at the moment, but apart from that everything's going well.'

Lucy laughed and then sniffed. 'Sorry. She does that. Are the girls OK? Andy just wanted…'

'I know. Actually I think it was a good idea, because they were really worried about him and they seemed reassured. I wish I could come and be with you, darling, but I guess I'm more use here. Is there anything I can do?'

'Cuddle Lottie for me,' she said, and then had to fight back the tears again.

'Hey, come on, you're made of sterner stuff than that,' her mother said, ever practical. 'I thought I'd change your sheets—he'll need clean sheets when he comes home. And someone's been in the attic, so I've changed those sheets, too, and done all the rest of the washing, and your father's taken the girls to school and then he's going to walk the dog.'

'Thank you, Mum. I don't know what we would have done without you.'

'Well, you aren't without us, and that's what families are for. You just sit tight, and let us know how it goes, and don't worry about the girls, they're OK.'

'Thank you.'

She finished her coffee, then couldn't suddenly bear to be so far from him, so she went back to the hospital and paced around his room.

And then the phone rang, and it was David. 'Lucy, I've got Andy here for you,' he said. 'We've done the craniotomy and the biopsy, and we've woken him up and he's quite comfortable, so we're about to go ahead with the surgery, but I thought you might like to talk to him.'

And then Andy was on the line, to her astonishment, sounding slightly drowsy otherwise but utterly normal.

'Hi, Luce. How're you doing?'

'Oh—I'm fine,' she said with a little gasp. 'I can't believe I'm talking to you. How are you? How is it?'

'OK. It's a bit surreal. There's a frame holding my head still, and I can't see anything, but I can hear them all talking and I gather they're inside now and they're about to start debulking it, I think. They're going to do some mapping, find out which areas do what, but I can't feel a thing. I thought it would hurt, but it's fine. Just—weird.'

'Gosh. It's amazing to talk to you. I'm glad it doesn't hurt. Are you really OK?'

'Yeah, I'm fine. It's good. Interesting. How are the girls?'

'OK. Lottie was spreading breakfast in her hair when I spoke to Mum.'

She heard him chuckle, and then someone said something and he said, 'Oh. I've got to go. They're going to start the serious stuff, so I have to count and read out loud and wiggle my fingers and things. I'll see you later.' There was a tiny hesitation, then he murmured, 'Love you.'

He hadn't said that in so long it almost took her breath away. 'Love you, too,' she said, and then the phone went dead and she sat down on the chair with a plonk and waited, his softly murmured words echoing poignantly in her head.

* * *

They updated her once they'd done the initial mapping to identify the functioning areas under the tumour, and again when the biopsy result came back.

She was in a little park when that call came, strolling aimlessly around and watching children kicking up the autumn leaves, and she rang her mother.

'It's benign,' she told her, and burst into tears.

'Oh, Lucy, that's fantastic! I'm so glad. Darling, talk to your father, I'm a bit tied up with Lottie.'

There was a slight scuffle, then her father came on the line.

'Hi, darling, I gather it's good news. How is he?'

'Fine,' she gulped, sucking in a breath and swiping away the tears. 'He's going to be fine. It's very deep, and it's going to take them a long time to get it all, apparently, but then it shouldn't regrow and he'll be fine.'

'And his speech?'

'I don't know. I spoke to him in Theatre before they started removing the tumour and he sounded fine, but I don't know how he'll be when it's over. It's just a case of waiting now.'

'Well, let us know when he's out. We're thinking of you.'

'Thanks. Give Lottie a hug.'

'Will do.'

She looked at her watch. It was nearly twelve. Four hours since he'd gone to Theatre, over three since she'd eaten anything. No wonder she was feeling shaky and pathetic.

She went back to the café and ordered another coffee, but decaf this time so she didn't end up with palpitations. She was close enough as it was. She bought a sandwich to go with it but she only picked at it, her appetite in tatters.

And then she went back to his room to wait, and almost immediately she had a call to say he was in Recovery and doing well.

'Is he talking?'

'Yes, but that will probably change in the next few hours,' David told her. 'We had a bit of a struggle to get the last part out, so it might take a while for him to recover completely, but I'm hopeful he won't have any lasting deficit. He'll probably get worse in the next few days, and then he'll slowly start to get better. We'll see how he is tomorrow. I'd like to keep an eye on him for twenty four hours, but then I think you should be able to take him home some time tomorrow afternoon.'

'That sounds good,' she said shakily. 'Thank you, David. Thank you so much.'

'My pleasure. I'll see you both in a while, but he should be with you shortly.'

He was awake when they brought him back, but drowsy.

'Hi there,' she said, and he smiled slightly and lifted his hand.

'Hi,' he said, after a second. 'OK?'

'Yes, I'm fine. Pleased to see you. How are you?'

'OK. Tired. Very…long.'

'I'm sure it was. Why don't you have a sleep now? I'll be here.'

He grunted softly, his eyes drifting shut, and she sat there beside him and watched him sleep while the nurses quietly came and went.

She'd expected his head to be bandaged, but there was just a strip of dressing stuck on the suture line, a narrow channel shaved in his hair around three sides of a square, above his left ear and over his temple. At a glance you might not even notice there was anything amiss, she thought, especially since his hair was long overdue for a cut. Given a couple of weeks, it would be invisible.

'Will he be in pain?' she asked one of the nurses, and she shook her head.

'No, he shouldn't be. He will have been given something in Theatre so it won't be hurting him now. He should be quite comfortable, and he'll be discharged on painkillers. They usually manage very well post-op.'

That was reassuring to know. It seemed bizarre, impossible, that David had been inside his head, meticulously dissecting out that huge and threatening mass she'd seen on the scan images. Even more bizarre to know that it had been growing there for who knew how long. Had it changed him? Sucked away his personality? He'd certainly been different, but was that all down to the tumour, or something else?

Well, it was gone now, and only time would tell if that had been the cause. Whatever the reason, she was determined to get their marriage back on track. She knew it wouldn't be easy, but they would get there, she promised herself.

Come hell or high water, they would get there.

He slept off and on for the rest of the day.

David came to see him, and he sat up and shook his hand and seemed OK. Until he tried to speak, and then the words just weren't there.

'Don't worry,' David said. 'You were fine during the op, you didn't suffer any significant speech arrest while we were working, and you were talking well all through it, so this is temporary, OK? It's all still there, it's just a case of giving it time, and I think within a few days you'll be starting to see a real improvement. I know it's frustrating, but it's not for ever. Hold that thought, OK?'

'OK,' he said, David's words swirling around in his head, some of them meaningless. 'Wh—wha—whe...'

'When can you go home?'

'Yeah. Go—home.'

'Tomorrow, I think. We'll do another scan, and then

you can leave once I'm happy everything's as it should be. You probably don't want to go on the train, so you could either book a cab or arrange for someone to pick you up.'

He nodded, turning to Lucy. 'You—um—'

'I'll get my father to come. OK?'

'OK,' he said, sagging back against the pillows. 'Good.'

'Has Kate North been yet?'

'No,' Lucy told him. 'Will she come today?'

'Yes. She's got a chart with pictures of things that you can point to, so you can ask for what you want to help you get through these early days, and all sorts of other ideas. I'll page her, get her to come and see you, and I'll be back in the morning. You're doing really well, Andy. Hang in there. I'll see you later.'

He patted him on the shoulder and left them, and Andy turned away, but not before she'd seen the bleak expression in his eyes.

He should have expected it.

He'd been warned. He'd known it was possible that he'd lose his speech for a bit, but it was scary the way the words had just gone, vanished into thin air.

He was surprised he could think so clearly. Not in words, not really, more concepts. Feelings.

Frustration, relief, impatience.

Thirst.

There was a glass and a bottle of water on the locker beside him, but his right hand was being a bit uncooperative, and he didn't fancy his chances of getting the lid off.

'Do you want a drink?'

He nodded carefully, and Lucy came round to the other side of the bed, back into his line of sight, and poured him a glass of water. He lifted his right hand, changed his mind and took it with his left.

Bliss. It tasted amazing. Cool and sweet and clean. He drained it and handed it back, and she put it down and perched on the bed beside him.

'The girls send their love. I've spoken to them, told them you're all right and you're going to be OK. They told me to give you a cuddle.'

She leant forwards with a smile and put her arms round him, and after a second he lifted his arms and slid them round her, easing her closer so her head was beside his, her cheek against his right temple so that his nose was buried in her hair. It smelt of her shampoo, soft and fragrant, achingly familiar and oddly reassuring.

He only let her go when Kate North came into the room, and as Lucy straightened up he could see moisture under her eyes.

'Hi there,' Kate said, pulling up a chair as Lucy moved away to stand by the window, surreptitiously swiping the last trace of tears from her cheeks and staring out into the gathering gloom of the early evening.

The nights were drawing in, the days shorter and shorter.

Would he be talking by Christmas?

And would they still be together?

Yes. He loved her. He'd said so. She hugged the thought to her heart. Whatever was coming, they could deal with it together...

Kate gave him a chart.

He hated it. Hated having to point, but it beat lying there trapped in a silent prison where everybody else could talk except him. He could manage some words. Simple stuff, greetings and so on, meaningless things, but to ask for a specific thing seemed infinitely harder and absolutely beyond reach.

But he was alive. He told himself that, again and again,

over the course of the next few hours, but when the morning came the little bit of speech he'd had seemed to have slipped away and even thinking was harder. And his right arm was even less useful, so that Lucy had to help dress him when David said he could go home.

Her father came, and he sat in the front with the seat reclined, dozing most of the way, and then he heard the crunch of gravel and opened his eyes.

'Home,' he said, after groping for a moment, and Lucy smiled at him, her eyes misting.

'Yes. Home. Come on, let's get you inside and have a cup of tea.'

And then the girls were running out, slinging their arms around him and hugging him, the dog pushing in and licking his hand, and he felt his eyes filling and welling over.

Odd, because he actually didn't really feel any emotion, just a curious numbness. 'Tea,' he said, and the girls led him inside, one on each hand, towing him through the door and into the sitting room with Stanley at their heels, then Megan was climbing up on the sofa beside him and peering at his head.

'Careful, darling,' Lucy said, but he didn't seem worried, just put his arm round her and hugged her, Emily on the other side and the dog stuck on his leg, gazing at him adoringly. So far, so good, she thought, but not for the first time she wondered exactly what it would be like living with a man who couldn't communicate.

He wasn't the most long-suffering, and she didn't imagine for a moment that he'd be a good patient, but he was alive, he was going to stay alive, and he should get better.

One step at a time, she told herself. One day at a time, one hour—one minute.

'Tea?'

He nodded. 'Tea,' he repeated, but there was no answering smile, and she turned away before he could see the tears in her eyes.

Her mother was in the kitchen boiling the kettle, and without a word she put her arms round Lucy and held her. When she moved away, her mother searched her face and tutted.

'He'll get better. Isn't that what David said? That this is temporary?'

She nodded. 'Yes. It's just—I know it's crazy, but I wasn't really expecting him to be like this. Not speaking, maybe, but—he's not reacting to things, not responding, really, and his right hand's uncooperative—Mum, it's almost as if he's had a stroke.'

'Don't forget that the surgery itself is the equivalent of a brain injury,' her mother pointed out gently. 'It's tough. His brain is irritated, swollen, it needs time to recover from the insult. It's like concussion. He will be all right. He just needs time. Give him a few days.'

She sucked in a breath and nodded. Her mother was a nurse, and she'd worked in a head injuries unit for years. She knew what she was talking about, and these weren't just platitudes. She knew that, just as she knew everything her mother was telling her. But...

'Where's Lottie? I could do with feeding her to take the pressure off.'

'In her buggy in the utility room, sleeping. She dozed off on the way back from school and I thought I'd leave her, but she's had over an hour. Why don't you have your tea first and get Andy settled in, then you can feed her when she wakes up?'

She nodded again, picked up the tea tray and carried it through to the sitting room.

'Come on, girls, give your father a bit of room,' she said, setting the tray down, and they went and lay on the floor in front of the television. Stanley would normally have been there with them, with Megan draped over him, but he stayed by Andy's side, his head rested on his master's knee, eyes fixed on him.

Andy's right hand was lying on the dog's head, and she put his mug down in reach of his left hand, out of Stanley's way.

He just looked at her, meeting her eyes expressionlessly before picking it up. They didn't look like his eyes, she thought in surprise. They were just flat slate, dulled, without any of their usual expressiveness.

And then she thought of his eyes on Monday, when they'd gone out for dinner to the little Italian restaurant and his eyes had burned with that curious intensity. Now, it was as if the curtains had been closed on his soul, shutting her out, and she couldn't even tell if he was in there any more.

And she wanted to weep for him. For herself. For the children. For all of them.

Please, David, be right. Let him get it all back.

The alternative was unthinkable...

CHAPTER SIX

It was odd, how little he felt.

No pain, no anything, really.

Except tired. He was ridiculously tired, and after he'd finished his tea he got up and walked towards the stairs.

'Andy?'

Lucy was there, catching up with him in the hall and looking at him in concern. He wanted to tell her he was tired, but the chart wasn't around and he couldn't find the word for sleep, so he just closed his eyes. He could feel himself swaying, and her hand wrapped around his arm and steadied him.

'Do you want to go to bed?' she asked softly, and he sighed with relief and nodded, and she tucked her arm around his waist. 'Come on,' she murmured, and went up with him to their bedroom, helping him out of his clothes. His overnight bag was there, and he found his wash things and took them into the bathroom, and by the time he came out she'd closed the curtains and turned back the bed.

He crawled into it, closed his eyes in relief and crashed into oblivion.

'Is Daddy all right?' Emily asked, snuggling up beside her when she came back down, and she nodded and hugged them both. Lottie was stirring, and her mother brought her through and put her on Lucy's lap, and while she fed her, she sat there with her three girls and talked quietly to them about their father.

'He's going to be fine, but he might not be able to speak very much for a few days.'

'Did they cut his tongue off?' Megan asked, looking ghoulishly fascinated, and she laughed and shook her head.

'No, darling, but the bit of him in his head that tells his mouth what to say is very sore, and it just needs to rest for a bit and get better. You know when you fall over and get a bruise, it hurts for a bit and then in a few days it's all gone? Well, it's like that, as if his brain's got a bruise on it, and it just needs to get better.'

'Then will he be able to talk to us again?'

'Yes, he should be.'

She crossed her fingers behind Lottie's back as she said it, hoping she was right. 'So, tell me what you've been doing at school today. Did you have a fun time?'

'No,' Emily said, snuggling closer. 'I cried. I was worried about Daddy.'

'I cried, too,' Megan said, but Lucy wasn't sure if she was just copycatting. 'But we did painting, and it was fun. I did a picture for Daddy but it was wet so I had to leave it there.'

'I'm sure he'll be really pleased when you can bring it home,' she said, leaning over to kiss her. Lottie was standing on her legs and jumping now, and she held her baby firmly and smiled at her.

'You look happy. Did you miss me?' she said, but her mother just laughed at her.

'Of course she missed you, they all did, but they've been as good as gold, haven't you, girls? And they helped me cook last night. They were good girls.'

'They are good girls,' she said, hugging them all, and Lottie snuggled into her neck and blew a nice wet raspberry.

Her father looked at his watch. 'Lucy, darling, I hate to do this to you but we really ought to head off, if you're OK now? We just dropped everything and walked out, and I can't remember if I locked the back door, so we really should go home.'

'Of course you can go,' she said guiltily, putting Lottie safely on the floor and getting up to hug them both. 'Thank you so, so much for all your help.'

'Don't mention it—and keep in touch.'

'Of course I will.'

They hugged and kissed the children, and then her father patted her cheek gently, as if she was still his little girl. 'You take care of that man of yours. I know he's not always the easiest, but he's a good man, and I know how much you love him. You'll get there.'

She swallowed. How did he know there was anything wrong? She hadn't said a word—but this was her father, and maybe words just weren't necessary.

'Ring me when you're home,' she made them promise, and shutting the door behind them, she shepherded the children back into the kitchen, scooping Lottie up on the way, and set about cooking supper.

She was exhausted herself, more than ready to call it a day, and by the time she crept into bed beside Andy two hours later, she could hardly keep herself awake.

'Andy?' she whispered, and he turned his head and just looked at her. 'Are you OK? Do you need any supper?'

He shook his head. 'Y-you,' he said haltingly, and he reached for her, pulling her into his arms and resting his face against hers. 'Better,' he mumbled, and then she felt him relax again, his body slumping into sleep, and she snuggled down under the quilt, her head on his shoulder, and fell instantly asleep.

She was woken at eleven by Lottie crying, and she stumbled out of bed and went into her room, to find Andy standing by the cot stroking her and crooning softly.

'Come here, little one, it's all right,' she said, lifting her out and hugging her.

Andy handed her the feeder cup of water she'd brought up earlier, and she flashed him a smile and offered the baby a drink, then settled her again. She went down without fuss, miraculously, and they went back to bed, but Andy paused, sitting on the edge looking thoughtful.

'Are you OK? Do you need painkillers?'

He shook his head and pointed to his mouth.

'Hungry?'

'Mmm.'

'I'll go and raid the fridge. I'm hungry, too, I haven't really eaten.'

So she went downstairs and made ham sandwiches and tea and took them back to bed, and they lay propped up against the headboard, eating their midnight feast and sitting in companionable silence.

There, she thought. We don't really need to talk. Not all the time. And they snuggled down again under the duvet, curled together like spoons so she could feel his chest against her back, his arm warm and firm and heavy over her waist, his fingers splayed across her abdomen.

The last time they'd been in this bed together they'd made love, she remembered sadly, clutching at each other in desperation, one last frenzied reaching out before it might have been too late. How good it felt to be back here with

him, warm and safe and on the mend. Right then, nothing else mattered.

She closed her eyes, slipped back into sleep and didn't
stir till morning.

'Luce.'

She prised her eyes open and saw Andy standing over
her with Lottie grinning and reaching out to her from the
safety of his arms.

'Hello, little one,' she said, pushing herself up the bed
and taking the baby from him. 'Are you all right to carry
her? Don't overdo it.'

He just raised an eyebrow and disappeared into the bathroom, and she turned her attention back to the hungry baby.

'OK, OK, I'm here. There you are.'

She'd been surprised that her milk hadn't dried up while
she'd been away, because her expressing hadn't been aston-
ishingly successful. Maybe nature was cleverer than that,
and in times of such stress it knew when to shut down and
when to start up again. She'd been relieved to feed her last
night, though, and again this morning, and she sensed that
Lottie was relieved, too, to get her mother back.

Andy came out of the bathroom, disappeared down the
stairs and came back a minute later, and in the distance
she could hear the kettle.

'Is that a hint for early morning tea?' she said with a
smile, and for the very first time since the operation, his
mouth quirked.

'I'll take that as a yes,' she said, and changed the baby's
nappy and put her back next to him. 'Don't let her fall off
the bed,' she warned, and he rolled his eyes, so she grinned
and walked away, her heart lighter than it had been for days.

When she went back, Lottie was sitting on his chest,

holding his hands and beaming at him. He blew a raspberry at her, and Lottie grinned and said, 'Da-da.'

She stared at the baby, astonished. 'When did you learn to say that?'

'Da-da,' she said again, and Andy's eyes filled.

'Oh, Lottie. You clever, clever little girl,' she said, putting the tray down and getting back into bed beside them, delighted. 'Now, practise this. Mum-mum-mum—come on. Mum-mum-mum.'

'Da-da-da,' Andy said, and Lottie laughed out loud and grabbed his face, getting dangerously close to his scalp wound, so Lucy prised her off and cuddled her, then found her a toy other than her father to play with and handed him his tea.

Of all the times for her to come up with her father's name, there couldn't have been a better one, she thought contentedly.

Lucy didn't go to work that day, but she did on Monday because he told her before the weekend that he'd be fine. Somehow. A mixture of pantomime and pointing at the calendar and miming using a stethoscope.

She'd nodded and phoned the surgery and said she'd be in on Monday, and she'd gone, taking the children to school and Lottie to nursery en route.

'It's only for three hours. I'll see you soon,' she promised, and kissed his cheek and went, ushering the children out.

The sound of the door closing behind them reverberated around the silent house, and he leant back against the sofa cushions and sighed with relief.

So good not to have to think, or try and speak, or smile. He didn't feel like smiling. Didn't *feel* at all, really. It had been a hectic weekend, the children so pleased that he was there and seemed all right that they'd bounced excitedly around like puppies, and although it was wonderful to be home, wonderful to see them again and be surrounded by the chatter, he was exhausted, and he was glad they'd all gone out, Lucy included. Especially Lucy, maybe, because he felt she was watching him, searching for any slight sign of improvement, and he felt he was failing her.

At least his hand was improving. He'd been able to do up his shirt buttons today without help, although it had taken ages, but that didn't matter. What else did he have to do?

Nothing. So that was what he did.

The whole time she was out, he just sat there, staring into the garden and doing exactly nothing while outside the house the world all carried on as normal.

Would he ever be part of it, as he'd been before? Would he ever be normal again? He kept trying to reassure himself, but as the days had gone by and his speech hadn't returned, he'd grown more and more despondent.

Had David been wrong? Was the damage to his brain permanent?

Would he never be able to speak again?

Julie Harding, the local SLT Kate North had recommended, came that afternoon, after Lucy was home.

She'd been given a report by Kate, and she came armed with exercises and games and a whole bunch of stuff that just scared him because there was so much he couldn't do.

He could understand everything she said, could repeat it, mostly, but couldn't find it inside his own head without a prompt. But she came every day, and every day he got a tiny bit better, and in the meantime he had homework.

Ridiculously simple tasks, like matching pairs of words, copying words by writing them underneath—that sort of thing. And sometimes he even got it right.

He was boiling over inside, seething with impatience, scared because the longer it took, the more worried he was that it would never come back and he'd be trapped in a world of silence.

No. Not silence. Everyone else was talking, but he just couldn't join in, and he felt more and more remote.

Lucy didn't seem to know what to do with him, either. She'd tried to talk to him, but he couldn't respond so he'd just withdrawn, and she'd given up. He couldn't blame her. He couldn't talk to her, couldn't ask for anything, only demand it if he could find the word or failing that point to the loathsome chart.

He thought he'd go mad.

Some days he thought he already had.

It didn't really hurt. His scalp was a little sore, the whole area tender, but there was no headache, just a curious feeling of nothingness for the first few days.

At first he was ridiculously tired, but after that he was just plain bored. He couldn't read, or only with huge effort and he was saving that for his SLT homework. He could understand the television, but there was a limit to how much daytime TV he could cope with, so as a change from that he'd started walking aimlessly around the streets killing time. He had the dog with him, so at least it looked as if he had a purpose, but in reality he didn't.

And then feelings began to creep back in.

Frustration. Anger. Grief, for the loss of so much of himself.

And need. Need for Lucy. The need to hold her, to be held by her. The need to touch her, to kiss her, to take her to bed and make love to her until they were so close he didn't know where he ended and she began.

But he didn't. He didn't know how to ask, and she didn't

offer, and anyway, she'd kicked him out before all of this had happened, and they still hadn't sorted it out.

Maybe never would, if he couldn't talk to her. That ate at him like acid, but without words there was nothing he could do apart from bottle his frustration and his feelings.

So he kept his distance, and she kept hers, and he felt dead inside.

She was worried about him.

She knew a lot about expressive aphasia from her work as a general practitioner, and it was hard to tell just how much aphasics understood because it was hard to get feedback. At the moment, certainly, she was pretty sure Andy understood just about everything, which was good news. And before the op, only the high-level stuff had been badly compromised—like the research paper he'd talked about, which like so many of them could well have been impenetrable—so there was an excellent chance that he'd get it all back with time, along with his speech.

Knowing that, she was surprised that he'd shown so little interest in the television or radio. He just sat in silence, staring into space, or went out for walks with Stanley. He often did that—just went out for a walk, the faithful Labrador at his side. She had no idea where they went, or what they did, and she didn't like not knowing, just in case anything happened to him, but he seemed physically well so what could she do?

The incision had healed well and she'd taken the sutures out, but apart from that she hadn't really touched him. He just didn't seem to want her to, and that hurt.

She only had herself to blame, of course, because she'd thrown him out, but he was so withdrawn it worried her, so when Julie came on Friday morning she intercepted her while Andy was in the garden prowling round and looking frustrated as he waited for her arrival.

'I don't know what to do with him,' she said. 'He's just not himself, and I can't get him to try to talk at all—well, not just to chat. It's only basic, essential communication, as if he's afraid to try anything else.'

'He probably is. He's not a man who's used to failure, is he? And he probably sees this inability to speak fluently as failure, so he'd rather not set himself up to fail. Try doing it while you're doing something else together, like washing up or cooking or gardening. What's he like with the children? They're usually pretty good ice breakers.'

'Good, but he's not really speaking to them, he just watches them and looks sad.'

She nodded thoughtfully. 'I've got a game—it's great because it's not patronising. Lots of cards with photos on, and you have to put the things into different categories. It's got all sorts of levels it can be played at, and you could do it as a family. It's really good for the kids. It's in the car, I'll get it, but I would ask you to look after it because I've only got the one set and I'm supposed to be trialling it.'

'OK. Sounds good. I'm sure the kids will love it. Maybe they can do it while I'm cooking?'

'Good idea. You've got a brilliant family kitchen. What age is your eldest?'

'Emily? Seven. Coming up for eight.'

'So she's reading well?'

'Yes. She's quite good.'

'Great. I'll suggest it to him. Leave it to me.'

'Can't,' he said, when Lucy showed an interest in it later.

'It's funny that that's one of your best words,' she said drily. 'How about "yes" or "why not" or "try"?'

He just looked at her and walked away, picking up his

coat and letting himself out of the house, Stanley at his heels, and she sighed and dressed Lottie up warmly and pushed her to school in the buggy to pick the girls up.

And found Daisy there, picking up Florence because they had her most weekends. It was the first time she'd seen her since his op, and she suddenly realised how lonely she was feeling.

'Hi there,' she said, and Daisy smiled at her and hugged her.

'Hi. How's it going?' she asked, and Lucy shrugged, squashing the urge to cry. It would have been so easy to give in to it, but she wouldn't let herself.

'OK,' she said. 'Sort of. Physically he seems fine, he's recovered well and I've taken his sutures out, but he's a bit down in the dumps, I think, and he won't speak unless he absolutely has to. I think he's bored and fed up, and I can see that.'

'You ought to get him out a bit, start having a social life again,' Daisy suggested. 'Why don't you come for dinner?'

'I've got a better idea. Come to us. We owe you big-time for all the help you gave us over his op, and anyway, you haven't got a kitchen so it's a bit of an empty threat.'

Daisy laughed. 'True. OK. When? We're free this week-end—we're only having Florence tonight as a favour to Jane and Peter, and then they're having both children to-morrow night because we were supposed to be going out, but it's been cancelled, so we're at a loose end if that's any good?'

'Brilliant. Come at seven thirty. We should have the girls in bed by then.'

'Done. Can I bring anything?'

'Yes. Your sense of humour. It's a bit lacking at the moment at home.'

. 'Oh, Lucy.' Daisy hugged her again, and for the briefest moment she let herself lean on her friend.

And then Daisy was easing away, and smiling at someone over her shoulder. 'Well, if it isn't the man himself. Hi, soldier. How are you?'

'OK,' he said, and he smiled, but it didn't really reach his eyes.

Daisy wasn't fazed. 'Neat scar,' she said, peering at his hair with a grin. 'Amazing. Did they put anything useful in there while they had the chance?'

He gave a short huff of what might have been laughter, but he seemed to relax a fraction, and Lucy let out a sigh of relief.

'I've invited Ben and Daisy to dinner tomorrow night,' she told him as they walked home, and he stopped dead and stared at her.

'Can't,' he said, looking pressured and frustrated. 'Can't—speak.'

'I've told you about "can't",' she said gently, taking his arm and hugging it as he pushed the buggy. 'You don't have to speak, you can pour wine. That'll be useful.'

He did that humourless, empty little laugh again, and she wondered if it had been such a good idea inviting them, after all. Well, she'd find out tomorrow.

'What shall we give them to eat?' she asked, clearing up the breakfast things as he finished his coffee the next morning, the newspaper untouched beside him.

He shrugged and shook his head.

'I don't know, either. Any suggestions? Meat? Fish? Curry? Roast?'

'Curry,' he said instantly.

She glanced across at him, wondering if this was too big a challenge, because he still wasn't really reading and he might need to look at the recipe. And his hand was still a little shaky, although much better than it had been last week. Could he do it? One way to find out.

'Only if you cook,' she said innocently. 'I'm rubbish at it. You always do the curries.'

He shrugged again. 'OK.'

She cracked then, not wanting to push him too far. 'I'll help. What kind of curry?'

He frowned thoughtfully, squawked and flapped his elbows, and she laughed without thinking.

'Chicken curry?' she tried, and he nodded.

'Chicken. Chicken pas—um. And—' He broke off, drawing a P on the table. 'Pil...'

'Pasanda, and pilau rice?' He nodded, his shoulders dropping as the frustration eased. 'OK,' she said. 'And we can get poppadoms and chapattis—what about a pudding?' She pushed away from the worktop and fetched a notepad and pen. 'I'm going to have to go to the supermarket. I know we haven't got enough mango chutney and I think we're short of rice.'

And then she had a brainwave. There was no need for them all to go shopping, and while she was out they could try out that game. She scribbled a list, then straightened up and looked at him.

'How would you feel about me leaving you with the girls and going shopping with Lottie? Is that OK? Are you happy looking after them?'

'We'll look after Daddy,' Emily said, cuddling up to him, and he tucked her under his arm, kissed the top of her head and nodded.

'OK.'

'Why don't you try that game Julie left yesterday?' she suggested casually, and put it on the table. 'Here—Emily, you read the instructions out.'

Heart in mouth, she went off to the supermarket, hoping she hadn't caused havoc at home, and came back to find Megan and Emily kneeling up and leaning over the table, and Andy looking smug.

'Daddy's really good at it,' Megan said, sounding disgusted. 'It's too hard.'

'No, it's not, you just have to think,' Em pointed out, but Andy cut them off by tidying away the game and coming over to help her unpack the shopping.

She gave him a hug, and he hugged her back, holding on a second or two longer than she'd expected, and she tipped her head back and saw something new and different in his eyes. Something warm and interesting and much more like the old Andy.

Thank goodness for that. She'd been so afraid she'd pushed him too hard by leaving him with the girls to play the game.

She smiled, went up on tiptoe and kissed him, lingering for a moment, and then busied herself putting everything away, her body singing. That look in his eyes needed following up. Not now, though. Now, she had a supper party to prepare for, and the house was far from ready. But later...

'Right, you cook, I'll clean. Em, Megan, will you keep an eye on Lottie, please?'

It was good to see Ben again.

Surprisingly good, and he found himself smiling as Ben came in armed with two bottles of wine and a box of chocolates, dumped them on the table and shook his hand.

'Hey, Andy, it's great to see you,' Ben said, and hugged him briefly, slapping him on the back. 'You're looking good. How are you?'

He grunted and shook his head. 'OK—talking—not... great.'

'Well, that makes a change,' Ben said drily. 'I might get a word in edgeways. May I?' He lifted his hair out of the way and checked the suture line. 'Very tidy. Nice job.' He dropped the lock of hair. 'They've got a good locum covering you, by the way,' he added, 'but I think they miss you. It's all a bit quiet in there without your sharp tongue and razor wit.'

Andy rolled his eyes, for want of a better expression, and Ben chuckled. 'Come on, get the wine open. Working on the principle that there was some serious celebrating to do, we walked, so let's not hold back.'

Andy laughed, a real laugh that caught him by surprise, and got the corkscrew out. 'Here—you. Busy.'

And he turned back to the curry, stirring and tasting it. Ben followed him, dipping the tip of his finger in and sucking it.

'That's nice. Very nice. Did you cook it?'

He nodded.

'Can I have the recipe?'

'Not another curry recipe!' Daisy said, laughing. 'He's got loads. It's the only thing he can cook, so I hope it's not too hot. I don't want to have the baby tonight, it's not due for weeks yet.'

Andy shook his head. 'No. Um...' He found himself tracing the letter on the worktop. 'Pas...' he groped, and then Ben bailed him out.

'Pasanda? It is mild, Daisy, and you'll love it. In fact, it's probably nicer than mine, dammit.'

'Oh, perish the thought,' Daisy said, laughing, and then pushed a wine bottle towards him. 'I thought you'd been given a job? I think Andy's tongue's hanging out there, and I could do with a drink if you've got anything soft.'

* * *

'That was a great evening. The curry was gorgeous. Thank you, darling.'

'W-wel—' Damn, where was the word?

'Welcome?' she offered, and he nodded.

'Yeah. Welcome. Good idea.'

She smiled. 'I thought so. Time for bed?'

He looked at the kitchen table. She'd cleared it at some point, probably while she'd been making the coffee and he'd been talking to Ben. Or the other way round, more likely. Whatever, the dog couldn't get to any leftovers, the dishwasher was on and there was nothing to stop them going to bed.

He felt curiously hesitant, though. Not that he wasn't tired, but she looked lovely tonight, and he wanted her. Wanted to touch her, to hold her, to kiss away the little streak of chocolate on her lip and then plunder her mouth. He just didn't know how to say so without sounding clumsy and awkward.

'Come on,' she said gently, taking him by the hand and leading him towards the stairs.

'Dog?' he said, but she just shook her head.

'I put him out a few minutes ago. He's fine.'

He followed her, letting her lead him into the bedroom and close the door quietly but firmly behind them.

Then she turned and went up on tiptoes and pressed her mouth softly to his.

'Thank you,' she murmured.

'Why?' he asked, for want of a better word.

'For cooking for us. For having a go, and doing it so well, and not just saying "can't".'

She pulled his shirt out of his trousers and unbuttoned it, slowly and systematically, and when she looked up, her eyes were warm and welcoming, and it turned out he didn't have to say anything, didn't have to ask.

His heart pounding slightly, he cupped her face in his hands, bent his head and took her mouth in a long, slow, lingering kiss that left both of them wanting more.

'Luce,' he murmured, nuzzling her neck, trailing his tongue over the hollow of her throat where he could feel her pulse picking up, too. He slid his hands up under her top, cupping her breasts, soft and warm, achingly right in his hands. He slipped the catch on her bra and moved it out of the way, letting the weight of them fill his palms, and she moaned softly and slid the shirt off his shoulders.

He let it drop to the floor behind him, then peeled off her top over her head and unfastened her jeans, sliding them down over her hips, snagging the little lace knickers on the way and pushing her gently back onto the edge of the bed.

She sat down and obediently picked up her feet, one at a time, so he could strip her jeans away, and then she reached for his belt. It was ages since they'd done this, slowly and deliberately seduced each other, and she found herself smiling.

'What?' he asked, and she looked up and met his eyes.

'Nothing. It's just nice.'

'Mmm.'

She hooked her thumbs in his waistband and pulled his trousers down, then he bent and kicked them off, heeling off his shoes at the same time and kicking them out of the way. Slowly, deliberately, she peeled down the soft, clingy jersey shorts, and he pushed her gently backwards onto the bed, lifted her legs and tucked them under the quilt and slid in beside her, drawing her back into his arms.

His mouth found hers, and she threaded her fingers through his hair and then froze.

'Oh—did I hurt you?'

'No.'

'Sure?' She levered herself up on one elbow and leant

over him, pressing her lips to his hair, resting her cheek against the side of his head over the healed wound.

His hands slid up her back, warm and firm, and he eased her away and found her mouth again, and she forgot about his surgery, forgot about everything except lying there in the arms of the man she loved.

He knew just how to touch her, when to go slow, how to keep her hanging on until she was sobbing with frustration, and then how to set her free, timing it perfectly so they fell apart together, clinging to each other, then coming slowly back to earth with soft stroking touches, tender caresses, light, lingering kisses.

'Nice,' he said drowsily, and then he rolled to his back, pulled her into the crook of his arm and drifted off to sleep.

CHAPTER SEVEN

He slept better that night than he'd slept since his operation.

Amazingly, so did Lottie. Lucy crept out of bed and took her downstairs when she woke at six, put the kettle on, let the dog out of the kitchen and curled up on the sofa to feed the baby.

A few minutes later she realised that Stanley had disappeared, and she took Lottie upstairs and found the dog installed on the bed, licking Andy's hand vigorously and trying to look cute.

'Stanley,' she said warningly, and his tail wriggled guiltily as he slid off the bed.

'Sorry,' Andy said, looking every bit as guilty, and she shook her head and laughed.

'You're both naughty. No dogs upstairs. Here, cuddle Lottie,' she said, and handing his daughter over, she took Stanley back down, fed him and let him out into the garden while she made the tea, then she shut him and his wet paws in the utility room again and went upstairs to find Emily and Megan on the bed, too.

She went back down, brought them up drinks and climbed back into bed.

'When did we last do this?' she asked him, and he shrugged.

'Ages,' he said eventually, and she nodded.

'So, girls, what do you want to do today?'

It was predictable. Megan wanted to feed the ducks, Emily wanted to play the game Julie had lent them so she could see if she could win, and Lottie had what she wanted. She was busy pulling hairs out of Andy's chest and making him wince, but he didn't really seem to care and she thought he probably had what he wanted, too.

His family, all around him, and for once the time to enjoy them without guilt.

He looked up at her and smiled, and she knew she was right. If only he could keep it up when he went back to work, she thought, but that was a long way away and in the meantime there were ducks to feed and games to play.

'Can we have bacon and eggs for breakfast?' Em asked, and Andy looked hopeful.

'Andy, what do you want?' she asked, not letting him get away with that, and he just smiled knowingly.

'Bacon. Egg. Um—' He turned his hand sideways and chopped it down, then pressed an imaginary button.

'Toast!' Emily said victoriously. 'Daddy wants toast.'

'Tea or coffee?'

'Coffee. And marm...marma...'

'Marmalade!'

'Em, you have to let Daddy say the words,' she said gently. 'It just takes him a bit longer. I tell you what, why don't you say the beginning of what you want, and let him guess?'

'OK. Saus.'

'Sausages,' he said after a moment, and Emily clapped her hands and bounced on the bed.

'Well done! And tom.'

'Tomato.'

'Mummy, what do you want?'

'Pain au...'

'Chocolat,' he finished, the hesitation barely perceptible.

'You're getting too good. You do realise we don't have all of these ingredients?' she pointed out, but by the time they'd finished their tea and they'd all washed and dressed, the mini supermarket round the corner was open, so she sent Andy and Emily off with Stanley and a shopping list, and Megan entertained Lottie in front of the television while she laid the table.

They came back with extras.

Mushrooms, and another bottle of milk, and, because they had no pain au chocolat, some chocolate spread and croissants so she could make her own.

He put the bag down on the worktop, came up behind her and nuzzled her neck. 'Hi, gorgeous,' he murmured, and she turned her head and beamed at him.

'What do you want?' she asked teasingly, and he raised an eyebrow and grinned.

'Insatiable,' she murmured, trying not to laugh, and gave him a job.

'I won!'

Andy sat back and folded his arms and frowned at the game. Beaten by his seven year old daughter, he thought in disgust, but then he caught Lucy's eye and she winked, and he just smiled and let it go.

He'd get his revenge in time. His speech was getting better by the hour, or so it seemed today, so maybe David had been right and once the inflammation had gone down he'd be back to normal.

He'd said weeks to months. Maybe it really would be only weeks, and it wasn't yet two.

Plenty of time yet, and in the meantime, he was rediscovering his family, and the joy of spending time with them.

He looked out of the window, and saw that the rain which had threatened earlier had gone, and the sun was shining weakly through the trees.

'Ducks?' he suggested, and Megan leapt to her feet, fed up with a game she couldn't win and wanting to be out and about.

'I'm carrying the bread,' she said, grabbing the new loaf and running to the door. He followed her, took it away from her and said, 'No. Old bread. And—coat.'

She ran back to the kitchen, grabbed the other loaf of bread and was back at the door, one arm in her coat, the other one struggling because the sleeve was inside out. He sorted her out, then put Lottie's coat on and tucked her in the buggy, by which time Stanley was at his side, tail lashing, whining softly in anticipation.

'She always carries the bread,' Emily grumbled, but Lucy had appeared with an empty sandwich bag and she split the bread, ending the squabble before it started, and they set off to the park.

'There's Florence and Thomas!' Megan yelled, and they ran over to the others, leaving them to follow with Lottie.

'Hi! I was about to ring to thank you for last night,' Daisy said as they drew closer, 'so you've saved me the trouble. It was really lovely.'

'Yes,' Andy said, frowning in concentration but still smiling. 'Great. Thanks.'

'Thanks?'

'For—coming.'

'Oh, Andy.' She hugged him, her spontaneous warmth bringing a lump to his throat. 'It was a pleasure. It was great to see you.'

'I want that recipe,' Ben reminded him. 'Don't forget.'

'I'll remind him,' Lucy said. 'Are you heading for the ducks?'

'Yes. Are you?'

'Of course. It was Megan's turn to choose what to do, and she always wants to feed the ducks.'

'Well, why don't we feed them together, and then go back to our house for tea? I'm sure we've got some biscuits of some sort, and then Andy can realise how lucky he is having a sensible house to look after!'

Ben just groaned, and Andy slapped him encouragingly on the shoulder. 'Idiot,' he said cheerfully, and Ben laughed wearily.

'Tell me about it.'

'Nice house, isn't it?'

'Night—night—um,' Andy said as they walked away.

'Nightmare?' she suggested with a wry grin, and he nodded.

'Yup. Nightmare. Nice. But—sheesh.'

'Yeah. See what I mean about ours? Manageable.'

He grunted, but he had a thoughtful look and Lucy wondered why. Surely he wasn't contemplating a renovation project?

'You don't want one like that, do you?' she asked, and he laughed.

'No.' Firmly, definitely, no hesitation at all.

'Thank goodness for that,' she said, smiling, and tucking her arm through his, she walked along beside him, keeping a close eye on Megan and Emily who were sharing the lead and holding onto Stanley.

Bless him, he just walked beautifully along beside them both, as good as gold. It was all down to Andy. He'd trained the dog from day one—but that was before everything had gone wrong.

She put that thought out of her mind. He was home now,

and although he wasn't back at work, he seemed genuinely different, and he obviously wanted to be with them.

And hopefully the change would be permanent.

'Going to—hos...' he announced the next day.

'Hospital?'

'Yes.'

She was getting ready for work, and he'd said he'd drop the girls at school and take Lottie to the nursery, so they were all up and dressed, but there'd been no mention of the hospital.

'What for? Why are you going? Are you all right?' she asked, going into panic mode a bit.

'Fine. See—Raj and—James.'

'Oh. OK. Have a good time.' She kissed them all good-bye, then kissed him again. 'I'll see you later. You might get something nice for lunch.'

'OK.'

He dropped the girls off, took Stanley to the park and then home, and walked to the hospital. He hadn't been there since he'd walked home two weeks ago exactly, almost to the hour, and he felt a shiver of unease.

What would it be like going back?

Difficult, was the answer. He went to the Neurology clinic and asked to speak to Raj. Well, he managed his name, but not much else, which wasn't really helpful, and because the receptionist didn't know him and he couldn't explain, she was reluctant to disturb him.

'He's consulting,' she said. 'When he's free I'll see if he can fit you in. What's your name?'

'Andy. Andy—Gall—Galla...'

Raj came out of his consulting room at that moment, and he saw Andy standing there and came straight over. 'Andy, how are you? How's it going?'

He sighed with relief and frustration. 'OK. Not—not great.'

'I wouldn't say that. Come on in.' He took him into his room and sat him down. 'I've had a report from David Cardew, and I would say you're doing well. It sounds as if it was pretty extensive.'

He nodded. 'Yes. But—slow.' Hell, he was worse, because he was trying to pass on precise information, not just chat, and it was much more challenging. 'Speech—slow.'

'He said you had speech loss after the op, but he's very confident it's transient.'

'Good. Doing—head in,' he said, stumbling over every word, and then laughed wryly. 'Raj—thank you.'

'You don't need to thank me. I'm glad I was able to help. Have you been down to the ED yet? They miss you.'

'Ben—said.'

'Ben?'

Oh, damn. He couldn't remember his name. 'Um—babies,' he groped, and Raj nodded.

'Walker.'

'Yeah. Ben Walker. Going—now to ED.'

'Good, they'll be pleased to see you. How's the SLT going?'

He nodded. 'OK. Slow. All slow.'

Raj smiled. 'You're too impatient, Andy. Enjoy the holiday. Have fun with the kids. They grow up all too fast.'

He nodded again. They did. It seemed like minutes since Lucy had told him she was pregnant, and Lottie was eight months old now. Eight months old, and could say 'Da-da'. That was worth all of this. He just needed to remind himself from time to time.

He said goodbye to Raj, and walked over to the ED.

And was mobbed.

He didn't need to speak. They probably all knew he

couldn't, really, but it was amazing to see them, and he was hugged and kissed by nurses who under normal circumstances would have given him a wide berth, and slapped on the back by the lads.

And then James, the clinical lead, dragged him off to his office and gave him a coffee and told him how much they missed him.

'We want you back, but we know it's going to be a while,' he said.

'Want to come, but—' It was pointless trying to say any more. Those few words were enough to underline quite clearly his inadequacy. 'How—locum?'

'OK. Good. Not as good as you, of course.'

'Of course,' he repeated drily, if a little slowly.

They swapped grins, and then James' pager went off, so he followed him and stood outside Resus looking in and feeling swamped by frustration. He could see from here what was wrong, what was needed, knew exactly what to do, he just couldn't *tell* anyone.

And until he could, he'd be a danger to his patients.

James glanced up, and he smiled at him and lifted his hand and walked away, leaving them to it.

There was no sign of him when she got home with Lottie, and the dog was missing.

It might have meant nothing, but she had a bad feeling about it. Apart from anything else, he'd said he'd pick something up for lunch for them, and so she'd been expecting him to be there. She scoured the house for a note, then realised he probably couldn't write her one.

He'd gone to the hospital.

Had one of his friends dragged him off to the café for lunch? Unlikely. They all seemed to be too busy for lunch, but Lottie was getting grizzly, so she opened the baby a jar of food and was spooning it into her when she heard the utility room door open.

'No!'

He followed the sodden, muddy dog into the kitchen with an apologetic wince. 'Sorry. Door open.'

'That's OK. Are you all right?'

He ignored that, stared at her and swore softly. 'No lunch. Sorry.'

There *was* something wrong, she knew it now. 'Don't worry. We'll go to the pub. I'm just giving Lottie something, and she can come with us and have a nap in her buggy. They won't be busy.'

He nodded, but he didn't look overjoyed, just took the dirty dog back out to the utility room and came back a few moments later without him. 'Muddy.'

'He is. Where did you go?'

He frowned. 'Trees,' he said, when the word he was looking for evaded him. So frustrating. He was ready to punch the walls, but it wouldn't help.

'The spinney?'

'Yeah. Spinney,' he repeated, trying to rebuild the memory for that word, but it didn't work like that, he knew.

'Right, little monkey, let's clean you up and you can have pudding in the pub.' She made a bottle quickly, threw it in the changing bag with a pot of apple and mango puree, and pulled on her coat. 'Coming?'

He'd taken off his coat, but it was his dog-walking coat and she saw he was swapping it for a thick fleece. He put the buggy in the boot, then automatically went to the driver's side of the car. She saw him grit his teeth as he went back to the passenger side and got in, and she wondered what had happened, because he'd been fine that morning.

'How did you get on at the hospital?' she asked him when they were settled by the fire in the pub.

He stared out of the window at the sea surging against the breakwaters off the prom, and sighed. 'OK. Saw Raj.'

'Did you thank him?'

He nodded. 'Saw James. Everyone was—nice.' More than nice, but how to say it?

'And?' she prompted, sensing more.

'So stupid,' he said softly, his voice taut. 'Watched them—Resus—know everything, but just—can't.'

'Oh, Andy. You will be able to. Darling, it's only two weeks tomorrow since the operation. You're much better than you were. The words are starting to come, much better. And your hand's fine now. It's such early days. Just enjoy it—treat it like a holiday.'

'What Raj said. Holiday. But not, is it? Not holiday. And—what if...?'

'Andy, no. Don't start thinking like that. Just take each day as it comes. Starting right now. Lottie needs pudding. I think the ideal person to give it to her is the only person whose name she can say.'

And she handed the pot and the spoon to him, and went off to order their meal.

'Da-da-da,' Lottie said, smacking her hands on the tray of the high chair, and he stared at her, this miracle that was their child, and gave up. Maybe everyone was right. Maybe he should just enjoy the holiday, take it day by day and have fun, and let his speech take care of itself.

'Good girl,' he said, ripping the foil top off the dessert and dipping the spoon in it. 'Open.'

She opened her mouth, like a baby bird with a gaping beak, and he spooned yellow gloop into it and felt glad to be alive.

Well, something had changed, she thought, threading her way back through the tables.

Lottie was beaming and covered in pudding, and Andy was smiling at her and laughing and scooping the drips off her chin with every appearance of enjoyment.

'Da-da,' Lottie said, and he grinned, and she smiled.

That was it. Bless her, Lottie had charmed him out of his grumps and made him smile, and she could have scooped her up and hugged her, but she was covered in yellow slime and Lucy was wearing one of her few decent jumpers.

'Have you two spread that quite far enough?' she asked mildly, plucking a baby wipe from the packet and swiping it over her face. Two minutes later she was clean as a whistle, out of the high chair and snug in Andy's arms, having her bottle, so Lucy settled back and picked up her fizzy water and watched them.

It was good to see him with Lottie. He'd spent far too little time with her, and she adored him. Maybe there was truth in the saying that absence made the heart grow fonder.

'I ordered you fish and chips.'

He shot her a smile. 'Good. Brain—food.'

She laughed. 'Not when it's in batter,' she said drily, but there were times to worry about Omega 3 and times to have fun, and today was definitely the latter.

'I've got something to tell you,' she remembered. 'I saw a man today—a Mr Darby. He said you treated his mother two weeks ago in the ED, and she died. It was on the Sunday of the storm, just after we got home from my parents, I suppose, the day Raj saw you. He lost both his parents when a tree fell on their car, his father in the car and his mother in the hospital later. He recognised the name and asked if we were related, and I said yes, and he told me he'd wanted to thank you, but you weren't there. He said he'd been told you'd gone off sick, but that you'd apparently worked really hard on her.'

'Jean,' he said, remembering her face, remembering the

worry she'd felt about her husband. Remembering the clus-
ter of rings on her finger. 'Who—told him?'

'One of the nurses spoke to him. She said you were holding her hand, stroking it and trying to soothe her, and that
you wouldn't give up and they had to stop you.'

He hadn't wanted to stop. He'd held her hand, seen the
rings, and he'd felt a huge wave of sadness when she'd died.

'Last patient,' he said. 'Head—injury. Raj came.'

'And took you away for a CT scan, which is why you
didn't see the relatives.'

He nodded. 'Sad. Both parents. Like me. Maybe—better
together.'

'Better that they'd gone together, like yours did?'

He nodded.

'Her son thought so. He said she would have been lost
without him. They'd been married for fifty seven years.'

'Wow. Long time.'

'It is. I told him I'd pass it on to you. He asked how you
were.'

'What'd you say?'

'I told him you were getting better.'

He nodded slowly, and then smiled, glancing down at
Lottie in his arms. She'd fallen asleep, her arm flopped out
to the side, head lolling, and he eased her into the buggy
without waking her.

He was getting better.

And he would be a doctor again.

One day.

Julie came at three, just a few minutes after they were
home, and Lucy left them to it and went to get the girls.
She took the car, because Lottie was asleep in her cot and
might not stay there, and she didn't want to be out long,
and when they got back she heard voices upstairs.

'She's lovely. How old is she?'

'Eight months.'

'And is her name Lottie, or is that short for something?'

'Charlotte,' he told her, his voice carrying clearly. 'Liked—Lottie, though. No, Lottie. Keep still.'

He was changing her nappy, Lucy realised, and she was on the point of running upstairs to take over when she realised he was talking with less hesitation. Still slowly, a little haltingly, but almost properly. And he'd been better at lunch, once he'd relaxed.

Progress. Tiny steps but each one was massive progress, and they were happening hour by hour as his brain recovered. Overwhelmed, she went into the cloakroom, shut the door and put her hand over her mouth to stifle a little sob.

He was getting better. He was.

Finally, after two weeks of painfully slow progress, he was getting better, and the relief was immense. She hadn't realised how wound up she'd been, how desperately worried for him. For all of them, really, because if he'd stuck at that, he would have been really difficult to live with.

Thank goodness she'd never have to find out just how difficult.

She came out of the cloakroom just as they came downstairs, Lottie in his arms smacking his face with her hands and laughing, and she caught Julie's eye and smiled.

Julie gave her the thumbs-up, and she nodded. So it wasn't her imagination.

Unable to stop the smile, she veered off into the kitchen, put the kettle on and made a celebratory cup of tea.

Better, he realised, didn't mean cured.

Emily needed help with her reading, and Lucy was upstairs with Lottie, changing her nappy.

'Can't—do it,' he said, hating the admission, seething

with frustration, because it was so simple, so ridiculously damned easy, and Emily looked crestfallen.

'Never mind,' she said gently, climbing onto his lap and hugging him. 'Mummy will help me.'

He hugged her back, his eyes stinging with tears. He wanted to help her, wanted to be the one to do it, otherwise what was the point of him being there at all?

Being anywhere?

'Hey. What's up?'

He looked at Lucy, her face creased in concern, and he lifted Emily off his lap and walked away. He could hear her explaining, the words coming so easily to her, and Lucy's murmured response sounded reassuring and comforting.

He wanted to reassure and comfort—wanted not to have caused the need for that reassurance in the first place.

'Andy?'

He was in his study, the room which had always been his retreat, only now it felt like a torture chamber, filled with things he couldn't understand or deal with. Including Lucy.

She closed the door softly behind her and slid her arms around his waist. 'What's up, darling?'

'Em needed—reading. Couldn't—'

He let out a growl of frustration and slammed his hand into the wall, and Lucy let him go and came round in front of him.

'Hey, come on. David said it would take time.'

'Want to help,' he said, his eyes stinging again, and she made a soft sound of comfort and went up on tiptoe, drawing his head gently down and kissing him. Her lips were soft and warm and yielding, and he sank into the kiss, hating that he was so needy and yet absorbing the comfort she offered because he was so lonely and isolated.

'So much—want to say,' he mumbled.

'I know. It'll keep. Be patient.'

'Mmm. Have to.'

'I'm sure we can find other ways to communicate.'

He lifted his head and looked down into her eyes, seeing not only the promise but also the sorrow. Not pity, he realised, but genuine sorrow that this was happening to him. To them.

He kissed her again, just a soft, lingering brush of his lips on hers, and then he let her go.

'Want me—bath girls?'

'Please. I've done Em's reading with her but I need to feed Lottie.'

'OK.' He kissed her again, just because it felt so good, and then he went and rounded up the girls.

His frustration was still there, but for now, at least, it had moderated to the point where he could deal with it, thanks to Lucy. And hopefully, if he could only hang on, it would get easier to deal with.

Over the next few days his speech improved hugely, and every little improvement merited celebration.

Sometimes they went out for coffee and cake, sometimes they went to the pub for lunch, and sometimes, if Lottie was napping, they went into their bedroom, closed the door and made love, then lay there tangled in each other's arms dozing or talking softly until Lottie stirred.

Bliss.

Then on Friday, while they were lying in bed in the aftermath of another stolen moment, she had an idea. 'You have to see David in London on Wednesday, don't you?'

'Yes.'

'Why don't we ask Ben and Daisy if they can have the girls for the night, and drop Lottie off at my parents and spend the night in London? Maybe go to a show, even, and then we can come straight home after you see him. I don't have to work on Tuesday or Wednesday, and it would be so nice, wouldn't it? I think we both deserve a treat.'

He stared at her for a moment, then nodded slowly. 'Yes. Lovely. If they don't—mind.'

She asked them that evening, and they didn't. None of them minded—not Ben and Daisy, or her parents, and least of all Emily and Megan who thought it was a brilliant idea going for a sleep-over in the middle of the week. And amazingly Ben and Daisy even wanted the dog.

'Ben's father's a vet and his childhood was overrun with pets, and he really misses having dogs around,' Daisy said. 'And we've always said it would be fun to have a dog, but we can't get one until we've finished doing up the house, so to borrow Stanley would be lovely, so long as he won't chase Tabitha.'

'No, he's fine with cats, he's terrified of them, and feel free, you can have him any time you want,' Lucy said, laughing, and hung up and told Andy.

'Great,' he said, and he smiled, his eyes lighting up in a way they hadn't done for ages. 'So—what show?'

'I don't know. Let's look on the internet, see what there is. What do you fancy?'

'Something fun,' he said, after a moment's hesitation. 'Musical? But not too big. Not noisy. Don't want noise.'

'OK.'

They found a show, in a tiny venue, a function room in a restaurant off the Kings Road. The ticket price included dinner, and it looked perfect. The only problem was that it was sold out.

'Ring,' he suggested.

She didn't hold out any hope. The act was hugely popular, cripplingly funny according to the reviews, and she didn't think they stood a chance, but someone was looking after them.

'I've just had a family group of twenty cancel, and I had eighteen people on my waiting list, so, yes, I can offer you a table for two, but you are so lucky.'

'I know,' she said, grinning and giving Andy the thumbs-up, and he just shrugged and made his 'I told you so' face, so she stuck her tongue out, paid for the tickets over the phone and then did a little happy dance.

She had such a good feeling about this now.

'OK. Hotel,' she said, coming back to the sofa and snuggling up to him at the computer. 'How about the one we stayed at the night you proposed to me? That's close.'

And full of happy memories.

'OK,' he said, nodding.

It was eye-wateringly expensive, but they gave them an upgrade to a room at the back overlooking the gardens, and threw in breakfast.

'Done,' she said, and paid, trying not to think about how long their savings might last if Andy could never return to work. He had critical illness cover, but was it good enough?

She stopped the negative thoughts. There was a lot of water to go under their bridges before they needed to worry about that, and for now she felt they both needed a treat.

So it was costing them a small fortune. So what? She didn't care about anything except Andy and his recovery, and if it helped to bring them closer together, then she was all for it, because he seemed to be holding something back.

Despite his willingness to make love to her whenever they had the chance, he still wasn't talking about *them*, wasn't talking about the future.

He was spending time with the children, much more time, and seemed to be doing his best to make up for all the hurt he'd caused in the run-up to his exam, but time with her seemed—what?

Less romantic than she'd like it to be? Less loving?

He hadn't said 'I love you' since she'd spoken to him in the operating theatre, and now she was wondering if he'd really meant it then or if it was just David's 'happy drugs' talking. Or because he'd secretly been afraid he might die, and thought he'd leave her with that last thought to cherish?

Or because he really did love her, but it had taken something that drastic to get him to admit it.

Why? Was he still hurt because she'd thrown him out? It was a possibility, but until he could speak fluently again, she didn't want to force the issue and frustrate him.

Maybe, though, she could use this time together alone to create some new, romantic memories, to set the tone for their future. Not family time, not family memories, but something special between just the two of them.

And maybe then, given enough provocation, he'd tell her again that he loved her.

CHAPTER EIGHT

THEY left the car at her parents' house in Essex, got a taxi to the station and caught the train into London.

It took them less than an hour door to door, and when they checked in, the memories came flooding back.

Lucy was busy at the desk, and he let her deal with it while he looked around the foyer. The restaurant was through there, he thought, the place where he'd proposed to her over dinner. He hadn't done anything crazy like go down on one knee, but it had still been pretty public once she'd let out that little shriek and flung herself into his arms.

Where had all the years gone?

'Hey, what's up?'

He stared around, then looked down into her gentle green eyes. 'Just remembering. So long ago.'

'It's not that long. Come on, let's go and find our room.'

It was lovely, on the inside corner of the L-shaped building, so that the window was angled and they looked down into a mass of greenery where the gardens of all the houses that backed onto the area were mingled together out of sight of the busy streets.

It would be stunning in summer, she thought, but even in winter it was green and fresh and calming, a sort of secret oasis in a desert of stone and concrete.

She turned to him, about to comment, and found him sprawled out on the bed watching her, his eyes almost indigo.

'Come here and lie down.'

'Are you tired?'

'No.'

'Oh. I see,' she said, smiling and walking slowly towards him, swaying her hips provocatively. He raked her with his eyes.

'Good.'

'Mmm. I hope so.'

'Complaining?'

That was a big word. It made her smile. That, and the idea that she'd ever complain about Andy's lovemaking.

'Absolutely not. Never.' She took off her coat and hung it up, unzipped her boots and put them neatly in the corner under the coat, then slipped off her trousers, her jumper, the thin silky vest top underneath, her heart pounding with anticipation. He might not be able to speak to her fluently yet, but there was nothing wrong with his powers of expression, and when she glanced at him she saw his eyes on her body, flames dancing in them as she peeled off her clothes one by one.

If she'd ever doubted that he still wanted her, the doubt went in that moment, burned away by the fire in his eyes.

He didn't take them off her for a second, just lay there, scarcely breathing, watching her as she undressed for him.

Lovely. Beautiful.

His?

Maybe. He hoped so. He really, really hoped so, but if things didn't improve a lot, could he ask her to stay with him? There was so much he wanted to say, so much they needed to talk about, but he just couldn't. A conversation as important as that couldn't be bungled by his stupid lack of words, and he knew it was sensible to wait until he could really say what he needed to say.

Probably starting with 'sorry'. Hell, he could say that now, but on its own it was hardly enough, and she had some apologising to do, as well.

But in the meantime...

'Come here,' he said again, gruffly this time, and she went to him, dressed only in the skimpiest lacy underwear.

He tried to sit up, but she put a hand flat on his chest and pressed him back, then slowly, deliberately, she unbuttoned his shirt, then slid his belt buckle free, her fingers taunting him as she unfastened his trousers and slid the zip down.

He'd kicked his shoes off, and she patted his hips so he lifted them and peeled his trousers slowly down his legs. His clingy jersey shorts left little to the imagination, and she made a soft purr in her throat and ran her hands back up his legs, skimming past his hips, then settled herself over him.

She didn't say a word, and nor did he, just lay there and let her torture him exquisitely until he couldn't stand it.

It didn't take long.

She rocked against him, once, twice, and he cracked, sitting up and taking her face in his hands and kissing her as if he'd die without her. Maybe he would. He didn't know, and he didn't want to find out.

She slid his shirt down over his shoulders and off his arms, and then pushed him back, trailing her hands down over his chest and easing away the soft jersey that was separating him from her.

He swallowed hard, his breath jammed in his throat until she shifted her hips and took him deep inside her. Then he let it out in a rush, his hands reaching up and drawing her down so he could kiss her.

The lace of her bra chafed against his chest and he groaned and cupped the soft fullness of her breasts.

'Lucy,' he groaned, and she moved, killing him inch by inch, the sweet torture finally too much.

He snapped, rolling her under him, plundering her mouth as his body drove into her, his hands seeking, finding, worshipping.

She splintered in his arms, taking him with her over the edge, and he dropped his head into the hollow of her shoulder and waited for his heart to slow and his breathing to return to normal.

Then he rolled carefully to his side, taking her with him, their bodies still locked together, and he held her close against his heart.

'Very good idea, that,' he said lazily, and she laughed softly, her breath drifting over his skin.

'I thought so.'

'What time do we—go?'

'Not yet.'

'Good. Little nap,' he said, suddenly drained, and slid gently into sleep in her arms.

The show was amazing.

They'd walked there from Kensington, hurrying a little because they were in danger of being late, but they were there in good time in the end.

They went for a simple meal of hot chicken salad with ciabatta twists, with a good Pinot Grigio and a wicked dessert with a million calories and enough chocolate even for her.

And as the desserts were served, so the act started.   •

She was worried at first. Andy had seemed tired after their impromptu lovemaking, and she wasn't sure if he would be able to keep up with the pace of the jokes, but he was having no trouble, and she hadn't seen him laugh so much in ages.

Or herself, come to that. She thought she was going to split her sides at times, and she saw Andy wipe tears from his cheeks at one point.

Fun, he'd said, his only specification apart from music. This was both. Witty, exquisitely observed, the songs were hilarious, the volume wasn't excessive and they couldn't finish their desserts because it was too dangerous to eat at the same time.

They drank the wine, though, and ordered coffee, and she thought he'd choke on it at one point he was laughing so hard.

'That was—fantastic,' he said, when it was over and they were walking back to the hotel, the applause still ringing in their ears. 'Really, really fantastic. Thank you.'

'Don't thank me. It was you who chose it, you who made me call them. I wouldn't have bothered, and I'm so glad I did.' She lifted her head and looked up at him, tucking her hand in his arm. 'Do you know that's the first time I've heard you really laugh since your operation? And it's months and months since you've laughed as much as that. It was so nice to hear.'

'It felt—really good.' He pulled his arm away from her and looped it round her shoulders, tucking her closer to his side, and they ambled back along the streets, passing Harrods on the way.

Their Christmas window display was up, blazing with light, and they strolled past, fascinated and enthralled.

'It's amazing. They really do Christmas,' she said, and found herself wondering what their own Christmas would be like.

'Not long now,' he said. David had said two months, maybe. That would take them up to the start of the New

Year. He wondered now if that was too optimistic. He was certainly feeling much better, but he was a very, very long way off being able to go back to work.

Financially, it didn't worry him. He was off sick on full pay for months yet, and when that came to an end he had good critical illness cover—his parents' fiasco had taught him that lesson. But from a personal point of view, he wondered what on earth he would do to fill the time. There was a limit to how often he could make love to Lucy, although he'd yet to reach it.

They arrived back at the hotel and went up to their room, the rumpled bed a teasing reminder of their afternoon's activities. He took her coat and hung it up, then drew her back against his chest, nuzzling the side of her neck.

'Tired?' he asked, and she shook her head.

'No. Do you want tea?'

'No. Just you.'

She turned in his arms, slid her hands up into his hair and pulled his head gently down until his face was in reach.

Her lips feathered softly over his, and with a quiet sigh of contentment he eased her closer and took the gift she was offering.

Their appointment was for ten and he had to have a scan first, so they went down for breakfast at seven, checked out at eight and made their way across London in the rush-hour scrum.

'OK?' she asked, glancing up at him as they walked in, and he nodded. He'd been relaxed last night, but today the tension was back and she wondered if he was worried.

He didn't need to be, but then he couldn't see his progress as she could.

First stop was an MRI scan to see how things were, and

then David greeted them warmly, armed with the results and a broad smile.

'Well, the scan looks great. How's it going? Speech coming back?'

'Sort of,' he said. 'Still hard. Worse if I—*need* to say something. Exact words—really difficult.'

'That figures. You've got a massive vocabulary, so if you're just winging it, there are lots of words to choose from so you can take the first one off the pile that fits. If you have to be exact, as you say, you have to dig deeper and that's what you're going to find. And that will get better, but it's what I meant by the higher level stuff. This will improve quickly, the everyday stuff, as your brain recovers from the insult of the operation. The harder things, the more specific, the most critical—these will probably take longer and they will have implications for your career in the short term. Have you been back to the hospital?'

'Yes. Watched them. In Resus. Knew it—all, David. But—no words. I couldn't—*tell* anyone. Couldn't dir... um...'

'Direct?'

'Yes. Couldn't direct. Couldn't give—instructions. Couldn't lead. It's my job—'

'OK. Let's just take you back three weeks. You could hardly say a word. You've just told me perfectly lucidly what's going on at the moment. This is huge progress, Andy. Huge progress. I think that tumour had been pressing on your brain for months, and you'd just learned to compensate. The pressure's off now, but it's a bit like a memory foam mattress. It takes time to recover, time for the imprint to fade. And you have to give yourself that time.'

He nodded. 'OK.'

'How are you feeling otherwise? Physically recovered?'

He saw Lucy shift slightly out of the corner of his eye, and shut the images of her in their hotel room firmly out of his mind. 'Yeah,' he said in as normal a voice as possible. 'Physically, fine. Still a bit tired, but OK.'

'Are you having fun? Getting out and enjoying life?'

He nodded, smiling at the memory. 'Yes. We stayed—last night in—hotel, and went to—show. Very, very funny. Really good. Laughed a lot.'

'Excellent. I'm glad you're laughing again. That's a very good sign. You need to do more of the same. Get out there and enjoy life and do things with your family. Lots of fresh air, lots of physical activity and then puzzles, crosswords, all the things the SLT is suggesting, and don't worry about it. You're doing really well. I'm very pleased, considering how tricky the surgery was, but I really wanted to make sure I'd got everything, and I have, so this is it. No more treatment, just recovery. And that's just a question of time.'

'Always time,' Andy said as they walked away from the hospital. 'Story of my life.'

'Well, you're impatient, and you always expect to be able to do too much too quickly, so it doesn't surprise me at all that you're being impatient now, but I'm glad he's so pleased. The scan certainly looked different.'

'Didn't it? Much better. Feels better. Didn't know it felt wrong, but it did. Odd.'

'I'm just glad Raj spotted it.'

'Wouldn't have been—long. Getting worse, quickly.'

'You were. I'm still cross with myself for not realising.' Cross and gutted that she'd thrown him out when he'd been so ill, when she should have realised, if she'd looked at it dispassionately instead of in anger, that there *was* something wrong. Something serious. 'I should have seen it—should have recognised it. I'm so sorry.'

'Don't. My head, but I didn't, not really.'

'No, I think you did, I think you were just in denial. And you were never there, so I wasn't talking to you very much, there wasn't much opportunity for me to notice the changes. I still should have realised it was more than just tiredness and distraction instead of sending you away.'

'Well, here now,' he said, pausing in front of a café and smiling wryly. 'Fancy coffee?'

She smiled up at him and tucked her hand in his arm, happy to stretch out this time alone with him a little longer. 'Why not?'

Lottie was pleased to see them, and Lucy was very pleased to see her, too. Nature, it turned out, wasn't as clever as she'd thought when Andy had his operation, and her bra was feeling really tight.

'Has she been OK?' she asked, settling down on the comfy chair in the kitchen to feed her while her mother made them sandwiches for lunch.

'Fine. She's such an easy baby, she loves everybody.'

'Yeah. She loves them in the night, too, usually. She often wants to play.'

Her mother gave a wry smile. 'Yes, she seemed quite happy to see me at two something when she woke and wanted a drink. She was pretty disgusted when I settled her back down again and left her, but she went to sleep in moments.'

'She does, the little tinker.'

'So, how was your evening?' her mother asked, and Lucy tried not to blush.

'Lovely. We had great fun. Thank you so much for having her so we could do that. Andy was going to come on his own and I think it was really worrying him. He's still not confident having to talk to strangers. He thinks they won't understand. He's got a card that explains that he can't speak fluently but do you think he'll use it?'

'He's proud, Lucy. He's proud, and he's not used to being inarticulate. He's probably the most articulate and eloquent person I've ever met, and it must come hard to him when he can't even answer the phone or send a text or ask someone the way.'

She nodded. He'd had that problem when he'd gone to the hospital and the Neurology out-patients receptionist hadn't known who he was or what he wanted. And it had taken him ages to tell her about it.

'Never mind, he's much better, so I'm sure it won't be long. And I'm glad you had a lovely time. You deserve it.'

It had been lovely. Wonderful. Romantic and funny and full of secret, intimate moments, but he still hadn't said those three little words.

Oversight?

Or something more significant. Maybe he didn't love her. Maybe he was happy taking all the sex she could offer him, but didn't really care about her one way or the other.

No. That was wrong, she was sure of it. She was just being silly, wanting it all on a plate, and she needed to worry about the important things and forget it.

They'd had a great time, he'd been told he was recovering well, and maybe that was it, maybe the consultation had been hanging over him?

Time, she told herself, but the mantra was wearing thin for both of them, and she just wanted everything back to normal.

She thought of the sparkling festive Harrods window they'd strolled past on the way back to the hotel. Less than five weeks to go to Lottie's first Christmas, but at least she knew she'd have Andy at home this time. Last year he'd been at work on Christmas Eve and again on Boxing Day, and the children had missed him. They'd all missed him.

This time—this time, she promised herself, it would be special.

So, it was down to him.

OK. He could do that. He knew the tumour had been removed completely and wouldn't regrow, so he could concentrate on his recovery, but in the meantime, until he could go back to work, he had to find some meaningful way to fill his days.

His SLT exercises had been a chore until now. Suddenly, they became a challenge. He tackled them as he tackled everything, head on and with gritted teeth.

Crosswords, puzzles, reading and writing exercises, and listening to people speaking.

The radio was the easiest way to do that, because he could be busy doing other things at the same time.

Like painting.

Lucy had talked about how glad she was they hadn't bought a Victorian house that needed work, because they hadn't even got round to painting the rooms in their own, but she'd had two young children when they'd moved, and a part-time job, and he'd just started in his first consultant's post, so they'd had bigger fish to fry.

Not now.

Now, he had nothing *but* time, and so on Monday morning, he started to decorate. They even had the paint for the kitchen in a cupboard in the utility room, so the first thing he did was strip everything he could off the walls, scrub them down with sugar soap to get rid of the film of grease from cooking, and then Lucy came home from work with Lottie to find him cutting in the paint round the edges of the doors and windows.

'What are you doing?' she asked, looking a little stunned.

'Painting?'

She let out a tiny, slightly puzzled breath and said, 'OK,' and then tried to put Lottie down. 'Um—Andy, where's the high chair?'

'Dining room.'

'OK. Um—did we discuss this?'

'Yes.'

'When?'

He shrugged. 'You got the paint.'

'Two years ago. Why now?'

'Why not? Nothing to do.'

Oh, no. Not again. 'Have you had lunch?'

'No.'

'I'll make sandwiches,' she said, looking round at her devastated kitchen in confusion. If she'd known, she would have made supper last night and had it ready to go in the oven, but as it was she hadn't, and it didn't look like her kitchen was going to be hers again anytime soon.

She retrieved the high chair, fed the baby a jar of chicken something, gave her some banana to mash up and spread in her hair and made a stack of ham, cheese and pickle sandwiches.

'Lunch,' she said, and he got off the ladder, to her relief, and came and ate.

'Good. Thanks,' he said, still chewing, and got up and carried on.

'Don't you want a cup of tea?'

'When it's made.'

She sighed, wiped the banana out of Lottie's hair and put her on her play mat with a pile of bricks. 'Want me to help?' she asked.

'No, you're OK. Play with Lottie.'

So she did that. She played with Lottie, kept the dog out of the way and she watched her kitchen turn from the fairly gaudy yellow it had been up to now into a muted pale putty colour that went much better with the tiled floor. With everything, really.

'That's great. Well done,' she said, admiring it when she got back from the school run. 'What do you think, girls?'

'It's nice. Daddy, can you paint our bedroom next?'

'OK. What colour?'

'Pink,' Emily said instantly.

'I want purple,' Megan said, and they started to fight.

'How about one wall pink, and one wall purple, and the others white? That will go with your curtains,' she suggested.

Andy just raised an eyebrow in disbelief and cleared away the tools. He still had the woodwork to do, but at least the kitchen walls were done.

'Utility next,' he said. 'Then your room. But no fighting.'

It was down to Lucy to sort out the squabble, of course. They ended up compromising on pale lilac for the window wall, paler pink for the other walls and the ceiling white. Megan's bed was against the window wall and Emily's was opposite, so that way they each had their own colour.

'I want my own room,' Emily said to her later when she was clearing up after supper. 'I don't want to share. I don't like purple.'

'Well, that's tough. It's only a bit of purple, and the spare room's for when Grannie and Grandpa come to stay, or your cousins.'

'But they can go in the attic.'

'No, they can't. You can both go up there and have your own room when you're older. For now, I want you and Megan together on the same floor as us, OK?'

'OK. But I want it pink.'

'No. You have to compromise. We've talked about this. It's only one wall, Em. You'll cope. Where's your father? Do you think he'd like to read to you tonight?'

'He can't, Mummy. You know he can't read.'

'He can a bit, or you could read the story and he can help you if you get stuck. You can help each other.'

'OK,' she said, brightening up.

But he was decorating the utility room.

She leant on the doorframe and folded her arms and stared up at him as he worked. 'Andy, the girls want you to read to them.'

'I'm busy.'

'And they're growing up.'

He opened his mouth, shut it and looked at the wall. 'OK. Do it later.'

He cleaned up his hands, peeled off his painting shirt and went up to the girls' bedroom. She followed, ready to step in if it all got too much for him, but it seemed fine. She heard the little shrieks of glee, and him shushing them so they didn't wake Lottie, and then she heard the soft, hesitant rumble of his voice.

Em had to help him with some of the words, and at one point she took over and then he had to help her, and then Megan read a bit, and Lucy sat on the stairs and listened to them and felt her eyes filling.

'Hey,' he said, coming to sit beside her on the stairs a few moments later. 'What's up?'

'I was just remembering you reading to them, the night before your MRI, when you knew there was something wrong but not what it was exactly. And you read them a million stories, and I was just sitting in the bedroom and fuming at you for coming home and sleeping in our bed while I was away, and you didn't say a word about what

was going on. I should have known there was something
dreadfully wrong—'

'Ah, Luce,' he said softly, and slid his arm round her
shoulders. 'Can't do this yet. No words for it—too much
to say, and want it right. But—it's good to be here.'

'It's good to have you here—so good. There was a time
when I really thought I might lose you—'

'Shh. Not going anywhere. Just need time.'

'You can have time. You can have as long as it takes.'

His arm squeezed her, and then he got up and carried
on down the stairs.

'Where are you going?'

He looked back up at her. 'Painting,' he said, as if it was
obvious, and he disappeared into the utility room.

She followed him. 'Want some help?' she offered, and
waited for the rebuff, but it didn't come.

He stared at her for a second, then smiled. 'OK. Great.'

'Back in a tick.'

She ran upstairs and changed into scruffy clothes, then
went back and helped him.

Well, sort of. It wasn't a big room, and inevitably they
got in each other's way, of course.

And then he cornered her, reaching over her head to
touch up a bit she'd missed, and when he looked down he
smiled.

'Got paint on you,' he said, rubbing a smear off her
cheek. She wriggled against him, and he felt his body roar
into life.

'Are you—distracting me?' he asked, stumbling over the
words a little but his laughing eyes more than expressive.

'Mmm. Apparently.'

He felt her hand slide down inside his jeans and cir-
cle him, her eyes alight with mischief and desire, and he
sucked in his breath.

'Hussy.'

'Mmm.'

The children were upstairs in bed, asleep, and there was nothing to stop them, nobody to see. He put the brush down and turned back to her, smiling, and finished what she'd started.

There.

It was finished. Two coats of emulsion on all the walls in the kitchen and utility, and tomorrow he could start on the girls' bedroom.

They washed the brushes and roller, changed into their night clothes and went and sat down in the sitting room with a glass of wine.

'Well done,' she said with a smile. 'That was a good idea.'

'Talking about painting?'

Her smiled widened. 'All of it. Especially *that* bit. But it does look nice. And it was fun doing it together.'

'Still talking about painting?' he said, and she laughed and punched his arm gently.

'Girls' room tomorrow,' he said, and her smile faded.

'No! There's too much to do before you can paint their room, Andy. It's full of stuff, and they need to sort it out. You can't just pile it all in a heap in the middle and sling a dustsheet over it.'

'Why?'

'Because they need to clear it up,' she repeated. 'They have to learn—if they want it painted, they clear it up and put their toys away. And anyway, isn't Julie coming?'

'Yes. Damn.' He sighed shortly, and rammed a hand through his hair without thinking and winced. 'I'll do it after.'

'No! Andy, please, listen to me! Where's the fire?'

He sighed again, a longer sigh this time, and slumped back against the sofa. Lord, he was tired. 'OK. Do it another day.'

'You do that. You need to pace yourself.'

'I'm fine, Luce. Don't fuss me. I'm bored. I can't do— nothing. Going crazy.'

'I know.' She reached out her hand and laid it on his leg. 'Why don't we do something else together tomorrow?'

'Like?'

'Taking Lottie swimming. She loves it, and it's much easier with help. She's a bit of a wriggler and she could roll off the changing mat and fall on the floor now. I can't take my eyes off her.'

'Can't change with you.'

'You can. They have family changing rooms.'

They did? He didn't know that—because he'd never been swimming with her? He hadn't, he realised. He had in the summer, when they'd spent a few days at Center Parcs, but not here at home in Yoxburgh.

'OK,' he agreed. It might be nice to go swimming and burn up a few lengths in the pool. He was getting flabby and unfit with all the sitting around, and he hated it.

He opened a puzzle book and tackled a simple crossword, but he couldn't think of any of the answers. Well, not many. Still, at least he could read the clues now and they made sense. He tried another one, then tackled the Sudoku puzzle over the page, but he just couldn't get it.

He was tired, he realised. He could have done it in the morning, but now it just defeated him, so he threw the book back on the coffee table, put his feet up and went to sleep.

Idiot. He'd exhausted himself.

Lucy sighed softly and went and made herself a cup of

tea in her smart new kitchen. It smelt strange, but in a good way, and he'd done a good job, but at what cost?

He really needed to learn to pace himself better, but he never had, he always worked at things until he'd burned out.

Well, no, that wasn't true. Before his parents died he'd been more relaxed, but since then he'd been—obsessive?

Strong word, but maybe the right one. It had definitely changed him, changed his attitude to a lot of things. Nothing was ever left to chance now, and she sensed it was a backlash from the chaotic and random childhood his parents had inflicted on him.

He'd always been a grafter, though, ever since she'd known him. It was just the way he was, but he needed to take it easy now. She'd have to keep an eye on him, stop him overdoing it in future. She took her tea back into the sitting room, curled up in the other corner of the sofa and channel-hopped until bedtime. Then she turned off the television and leant over.

'Hey, sleepyhead,' she said, shaking him gently, and he opened his eyes and stared at her blankly for a moment.

'Oh. I was asleep. Sorry.'

'Come on, it's time for bed.'

He got stiffly to his feet, his right arm and neck aching from the painting. He flexed his shoulder, cupping it in his hand, and she slid her fingers under his and rubbed it.

'You've overdone it.'

'Maybe,' he admitted. 'Swimming will help.'

'Or I can give you a massage.'

'In bed?'

'If you're good.'

He smiled lazily. 'I'm always good.'

'Cocky, too.'

The smile turned into a grin. Suddenly he wasn't feeling so tired, after all...

Baby-swimming, he remembered belatedly, wasn't really swimming at all.

Mostly it involved kneeling in the shallow water of the baby pool, swooshing Lottie back and forth in the water while she shrieked with glee and splashed her hands. And drank it.

Every time her face got close to the water, her tongue came out and she tasted it. And then a child jumped in and a tidal wave sloshed over her head and she came up smiling.

'She doesn't care, does she?' he said, slightly surprised, but Lucy just shrugged.

'She's used to it. We come nearly every week, if we can, and I bring the girls in the holidays.'

It was a whole other way of life, he realised, and he'd missed it all because he'd been at work. Crazily, he felt excluded, and he turned the baby in his arms and hugged her. She beamed and blew a noisy wet raspberry on his shoulder, making him laugh, and then he looked up and met Lucy's eyes.

The expression in them warmed his heart, and he gave her a slow, smiley wink. She smiled back and held out her arms, and he turned the baby round. 'Where's Mummy?' he asked, and started forwards, holding her out in front of him. 'Catch Mummy.'

Mummy dutifully made a scaredy face and swam backwards, but they caught her easily and Lottie squealed with delight and snuggled her little arms around Lucy's neck and hugged her.

It brought a lump to his throat, and he suddenly felt overwhelmed.

'I'm going to swim,' he said, and left them to it, retreating to the emotionless monotony of the big pool where he carved his way up and down until his muscles screamed and his lungs were gasping.

Then he hauled himself out and nearly fell over, his legs buckling slightly under his weight. He was astonished at how exhausted he felt, how incredibly heavy. He'd been deceived by the buoyancy of the water. So, so unfit.

He looked for Lucy, and saw her in the little café overlooking the pool. She'd changed and was giving Lottie her bottle, and he glanced at the clock and realised he'd been swimming for nearly an hour. No wonder they'd given up on him.

Guilty and frustrated, he changed quickly and joined them.

'Sorry. Forgot the time,' he said. 'Want a coffee?'

'Please. I didn't bring my purse, and I couldn't get your attention.'

She watched him as he walked to the counter and ordered their coffees, something he wouldn't have been happy doing even a week ago. So much progress, and yet he seemed curiously restless and unsettled since they'd got back from London.

Take the decorating, for instance. And the puzzles and crosswords—he'd become obsessed with them. Still, it was paying off in the improvement to his language skills, but the swimming? He'd been driving hard, pushing himself with every length, and she'd watched the frustration burning through him with every stroke.

Because David had suggested he should do puzzles and SLT and keep himself fit? Probably. And Andy being Andy, he was doing it his way—flat out. His parents had a lot to answer for.

She sighed and sat Lottie up, wiping a dribble of milk off her chin, and she craned her neck as she caught sight of him. 'Da-da,' she said, and Lucy smiled wryly and handed her to him once he'd put the coffee down.

'Your turn, I think,' she said, and sat back with her coffee and watching him bonding with his little girl while his coffee grew cold, forgotten.

CHAPTER NINE

'So WHAT was that about?' she asked as they walked home.
'All that power-swimming? Were you trying to kill yourself?'

'Sorry. I just felt a bit—crowded.'

Crowded? By his eight month old daughter? When he
was used to a frantically busy ED department? She nearly
laughed, but she was still cross.

No, not cross. She'd *been* cross, when he'd taken himself
off to the big pool to swim for ages, but when she'd gone
to look for him and seen the driven way he was tearing up
and down in the water, she'd been worried. And now he
said he'd felt crowded.

Was this why he'd been taking himself away from the
family so much, because he'd found it all a little uncomfortable?

'How, crowded?' she asked, unable to work it out and
not wanting to let it rest.

'I don't know. Just—emotional.'

And he didn't show his emotions easily, she knew that.
Especially in public.

'Hey,' she said softly, hugging his arm as he pushed the
buggy up the hill. 'It's OK.'

'No, it's not. I said I'd help, but I didn't. I just feel—I
don't know. Useless.'

'Oh, Andy, you aren't useless! Of course you aren't useless! You did a brilliant job of painting the kitchen and utility yesterday—'

'You were mad with me.'

'No, I was just a bit surprised, and worried for you, really. I didn't want you overdoing it.'

He had overdone it. He knew that. He'd overdone it in the pool, too, but he had to push himself. It was what he did, and he didn't know any other way.

'What if I don't get better, Luce?' he asked bleakly. 'What if I can't go back to work?'

'You will be able to! You heard David—you're making great progress.'

'Not great enough. Better, but not right yet. Nothing like.'

'You always were impatient, weren't you? You want everything done yesterday. It'll come. You just have to wait.'

So he waited.

He worked at his exercises, he listened to the radio while he painted the girls' bedroom once they'd cleared it up, and he started jogging again, taking Stanley out for a run in the morning instead of just a walk. He and the dog got fitter, the house got painted, but still he wasn't right.

'When can I go back to work?' he asked Julie one day after his SLT session.

'I can't say. It's not a straight line graph, Andy. You're working hard at it, but your brain won't recover faster than it's able to.'

'Christmas?'

'I can't say. Possibly.'

'But—unlikely.'

'Realistically, I think so. It's only three weeks away.'

It was?

That surprised him. He hadn't registered the passage of the days, but he'd seen Lucy dressing Megan up in something for the nativity play at school, so of course it was coming.

'You're getting there, Andy. You've made huge strides, and I'm impressed with how conscientious you've been. Don't get despondent. It'll happen when it's ready.'

If one more person told him that, he'd scream.

He showed her out, then went and found Lucy.

'About Christmas.'

'What about it?'

'Are your parents coming?'

'I haven't even thought about it,' she told him. 'I had thought they might, but that was before…'

She tailed off, and he raised a wry eyebrow.

'Before you kicked me out?' he said, the memory still raw.

She closed her eyes briefly and nodded. 'But now—well, I don't know. What do you want to do?'

'Stay here. Just us.'

'That would be nice. We hardly saw you last year, or the year before.'

'I'll be here this year,' he said, not as a promise, but because it seemed less and less likely that he'd be anywhere else at this slow and frustrating rate.

'Good,' she said, kissing his cheek as she reached up to a cupboard to put the mugs away. 'Talking of Christmas, do you want to go shopping? I haven't even started yet, and I'm normally done by now.'

Christmas shopping? He hadn't done it for years—two, at least. She'd got everything, including her own present.

He'd asked her what she wanted, told her to get it and last year he hadn't even wrapped it.

Deluged with guilt, he smiled at her. 'Yeah. Let's go shopping. Now.'

'Dr Gallagher?'

They were walking along the main street looking in the shops when the voice stopped them, and Lucy turned.

'Excuse me. I'm sorry to intrude, but—is this your husband, by any chance?'

Lucy stared at the man for a second, then registered. 'Oh, hello. Sorry, I didn't—yes, he is my husband. Andy, this is Mr Darby. I told you I'd met him. You were with his mother when she died.'

The man held out his hand. 'I wanted to thank you, sir, for everything you tried to do for my mother. Their car was hit by a tree and my father was killed instantly, but my mother was taken to the hospital and they told me you worked tirelessly to try and save her. You probably don't even remember her.'

He shook his hand, remembering another hand he'd held, frail and gnarled, with three well-worn rings on her finger, symbols of a loving relationship with the husband she'd just lost. His last patient—ever?

'Of course I remember her. She was a real lady. Very worried about your father. Kept asking for him. We tried, but there was nothing we could do, no more that could have been done. So sorry we couldn't save her,' he said gruffly.

'Don't be. Without my father she would have been utterly lost, and they'd had a good life—very happy. They'd always said they wanted to go together.'

He nodded. His parents had said the same thing. They'd had a good life, spent all of it having fun, and none at all dedicated to the trivial details like wills or bank records, but they'd died happy. Maybe they'd had it right, after all?

'Still tough, losing them both together. I'm glad you stopped us. I hate loose ends, but I was ill and couldn't talk to you.'

'Yes, they said. I hope you've recovered? I expect your wife's been looking after you? She's an excellent doctor.'

He smiled ruefully, touched by his concern. 'Yes, she is, and I'm getting there, thank you.'

'Well, I won't hold you up. Have a good Christmas with your family.'

'We will. And you.'

They watched him walk away, and Andy let out a long, slow breath. There was so much more he could have said, so much more he should have said, but because it mattered, the words had flown, yet again, like startled birds from a tree at dusk, and left him almost monosyllabic and stumbling.

Damn.

'Nice man,' Lucy said. 'His mother obviously made a real impression on you.'

He nodded. 'Mmm. Real lady, even though she was dying. You could tell that. Hard for the family, though. It's tough losing both parents, even if it makes them happy.'

'You found it really tough, didn't you?'

He nodded. 'Just such a mess, as well.'

'I remember. It took you nearly a year to sort out the paperwork.'

Which was why his affairs were so meticulously sorted, he thought. One less thing for him to have worried about in the last few weeks. Just in case anything unforeseen had happened...

They walked on, strolling past a jewellers, and he glanced in the window. They had a display of antique rings, just the sort of thing that Lucy loved. She didn't even look at the window, though, just kept on walking, talking about the children and what they should get them.

Well, he knew what he was getting her. Seeing Jean Darby's son had jogged his conscience, and tomorrow, while she was at work, he'd buy it.

Whatever 'it' turned out to be. He'd know when he saw it.

The shops were heaving, the good old Christmas songs being belted out in every one, and he found himself singing along. Odd, how he could sing all the words fluently, when he struggled to say them on demand.

A different part of his brain, Julie had told him, and it seemed she was right, because after they came out of one of the shops he carried on singing softly, and Lucy gave him a quizzical smile.

'You sound happy.'

He grinned, the plan forming in his mind. 'I am. It's fun. What's next?'

They managed to get most of the presents on her list, but not all, and the following day Lucy announced that she was going to a big toy shop on the outskirts of a nearby town.

'Are you coming?'

'No, don't think so. I've got to do my SLT and other stuff. You go. I'll have Lottie, if you like.'

'Sure?'

He smiled. 'Yes, I'm sure. We'll muddle through together.'

'You haven't seen my engagement ring, have you, by the way? I took it off in the bathroom last night when I was bathing Lottie and I can't find it.'

'No. I'll look for it. It'll be somewhere.'

In his pocket, but he didn't tell her that. 'You go, have fun, I'll see you later.'

'OK. Well, I won't be long. Two hours, max.'

'OK.'

That didn't give him long, so as soon as she was off the drive he put Lottie in the buggy and walked briskly back to the jewellers.

'I'm looking for an eternity ring for my wife,' he said to the assistant. 'She likes antique rings. We walked past yesterday and I saw some in the window, but I couldn't really look. I want it to be a surprise. It has to go with this.'

He showed her Lucy's engagement ring, and she took him outside so he could point out the rings he liked, but there were none that were quite right.

'I want—oh, can't remember what it's called. Smooth setting, no claws, like this one, so it doesn't catch on things.'

'Cushion set.'

'Yes, that's it.'

'In gold, or platinum?'

'Gold. Her other rings are gold.'

'We've just had one in that might answer. If you could hold on, I'll see if it's been cleaned yet.'

She went out the back, and reappeared with the ring in her hand. 'This is it. The diamonds are very good, apparently, so it's going to be expensive. I'm not sure if we've got a final valuation. Would you like to speak to the jeweller?'

He stared at it, a strange feeling coming over him. He could picture it on Lucy's finger, see her hand worn and old, the ring still there even though the knuckle had grown thickened with age. Would they still be together then, as much in love as the Darbys had evidently been? He hoped so.

'Yes, please.'

A man emerged from the back, an eyeglass hanging round his neck. 'I gather you're interested in this ring.'

'Yes. I want an eternity ring for my wife. I promised her one eight years ago but I just haven't got round to it.'

'Ah.' He smiled. 'Well, this is a beautiful ring. It belonged to the grandmother of a friend of mine and he asked me to sell it for him. He didn't like to part with it, but there's nobody in the family for him to leave it to; he said it was too beautiful to go in a drawer and he wanted it to be loved.'

He held it in his hand, stroked his finger over the smooth setting, turned it so it caught the light. 'I can see why. It's lovely.'

'It's a very good ring. A little worn, but nothing that can't be repaired. And the diamonds are flawless. Beautiful diamonds.'

They were. Even though they were cushion set, when the light caught them they sparkled like fireworks.

'What size ring does your wife take?'

'I don't know. I've brought her engagement ring with me if that helps? She wears it all the time so I guess it still fits.'

'Perfect. Let me check.'

It was the right size, and he just knew Lucy would love it. The price was irrelevant, and he would have paid twice as much. 'Does it need repair?'

'A little. It's been worn next to another ring and the shoulder needs rebuilding. The setting's a little thin and it would be hard to match a diamond as good as these if you lost one.'

'Go for it,' he said.

He paid for it, slipped her engagement ring back into his pocket and walked home. He bought some nice ham from the deli on the way past, and arrived back just as Lucy turned onto the drive.

'Perfect timing,' he said, the ring burning a hole in his pocket. 'I bought some ham. You make lunch, I'll sort Lottie out.'

He changed the baby's nappy, and then went into the kitchen just as Lucy put a pile of sandwiches on the table.

'I found your ring,' he told her, handing it to her. 'It was in the bathroom.'

'Really? I looked there. I must be going blind. Never mind. Thanks.'

'So, how did your shopping trip go?' he asked her, trying not to look guilty.

Well, was the answer. She brought two bulging carrier bags in from the car as soon as they'd had lunch, and they spent the next two hours wrapping presents and hiding them in the loft ready for Christmas.

'Right, that's all the presents done,' she said. 'Well, except yours. What do you want? Any ideas?'

He shook his head. 'Nothing you can give me,' he said, trying to smile, and her face fell and she hugged him.

'Oh, darling. It's really early days. Don't give up. It'll all be fine.'

'I know,' he said, even though he didn't. 'How about you? What do you want?'

She smiled a little shakily. 'The same thing as you. I guess we might have to wait a little longer for our Christmas presents.'

Except he had hers, or he hoped he did.

He'd been promised the ring would be ready in time, and he felt a tingle of anticipation. He couldn't wait to see her face when he gave it to her. He knew she'd love it.

He went into work the next day, and cornered James in a rare quiet moment.

'Can we have a word?'

'Sure. You're sounding better.'

'That's what I want to talk to you about. I want to come back to work.'

'Ah. Coffee?'

'Yeah. Shall we go to the café?'

'Good idea.'

They got their coffees and settled in a corner of the café out of the way of the other customers. 'So—you think you're ready to come back?'

He remembered his conversation with Jean Darby's son, the way the words had vanished, and shrugged.

'I'm getting there. I'm just not sure what I have to do to prove it. I suppose there are procedures—boxes to tick?'

'Oh, bound to be. I was talking to Occupational Health, and they said they'd need a report from your neurosurgeon, and another from your speech and language therapist.'

He nodded. 'What about if I come back under super-vision?'

'The same, I think,' James said. 'In fact, I'm sure they'd insist on it, at least for a month or so.' He sighed and stirred his coffee, then met his eyes again. 'Look, Andy, it's none of my business, but why are you rushing this? Why not just take the time and enjoy your family? God knows you're lucky enough to have one.'

He felt a stab of guilt. James was only two years older than him, but he'd been widowed for ten years, as long as he and Lucy had been married.

'I know I'm lucky, but what good am I to them if I can't work?'

James gave an ironic little laugh. 'I know you, Andy. You're nothing if not organised, and I'd be astonished if you don't have really good critical illness cover, not to mention substantial savings and a cast-iron pension scheme with guaranteed equity. If you can't work, your family will still be taken care of.'

He felt himself colour slightly. 'OK. Rumbled.'

'So go home, get well, enjoy them all and come back when you're ready and not before. You don't want to get back and find you're out of your depth because you've rushed it.'

He was right. Frustrated, but knowing it made sense, he went home and resigned himself to another few weeks of pottering aimlessly.

Or, he thought, he could do something about the garden. They'd talked for ages about having a bigger patio to take advantage of the sun, and even if he didn't do that, there were a million other jobs he could do out there.

So he changed into scruffy clothes, pulled on his boots and his dog walking coat and went out into the garden, secateurs in hand, and cut down all the perennials. There was a shrub that had grown wildly out of control, and he cut it back, too, and shredded it, and then another one because it looked out of balance after he'd hacked the first one back.

By the time he'd finished it was almost dark, the compost bin was full and the girls were home, so he went inside and sat down at the dining table to help them with their homework.

If he could do nothing else yet, he could do that, he thought, but it seemed they didn't need him. Homework was making sure their costumes were all ready for the nativity play, and that was Lucy's department, so he took himself off to the study and tried to read the paper that had flummoxed him before.

It was no better. In fact, it was worse, and in sheer frustration he shredded it, changed into his running clothes and took the dog out for a run along the dimly lit pavements.

It was a good job he did, because as he ran past the Walkers' house, he glanced at it and saw Daisy leaning on the front door, panting.

He stopped in his tracks and went up the path. 'Daisy?'

'Oh—Andy! Oh, I'm so glad it's you. I've gone into labour and I can't get hold of Ben. Can you call him for me? He's gone late-night shopping and he probably can't hear over all the Christmas jingles.'

'Of course I'll call him. What are you doing outside? You'll freeze. Where's Thomas?'

'Inside. I'd just put him to bed and I heard a car pulling up, so I came out to see if Ben was coming and it just hit me.'

'Let's get you back in, you'll be freezing.'

He led her back inside, told Stanley to sit and called Ben while she leant over the sink and moaned softly.

'OK, he's on his way. What can I do?'

'Nothing. Stay with me. It feels a bit—ah!'

'Daisy, don't do this to me,' he muttered under his breath, but it seemed she was, so he shut the dog out in the utility room and made Daisy comfortable on the kitchen floor on some towels he found in the airing cupboard.

She was kneeling up, draped over a chair, rocking and moaning softly, and he knelt beside her and rubbed her back.

'Oh, Ben, where are you?' she was asking, and he nearly laughed because it so exactly echoed his thoughts.

The last thing—absolutely the last thing—he needed was to end up delivering the baby of a colleague who was an obstetrician! But he'd done it before, and no doubt he could do it again, if the need arose. He just hoped it didn't.

'It's OK, Daisy, you're doing fine, just hang on,' he said, but she couldn't, it seemed. Unless he was mistaken, the baby was coming any moment.

'OK, Daisy, pant,' he urged. 'Don't push.'

'Got to push!'

'No. Just pant, little light breaths. Come on, you can do it,' he pleaded.

And then, just when he thought he was going to have to deliver it, he heard a key in the front door and Ben was there.

He took one look, rinsed his hands hastily and caught his baby as she emerged purple and furious into the world.

Redundant now, Andy left them in peace and went upstairs to Thomas, who was screaming in his cot.

'Hey, little guy, you've got a sister,' he said, picking him up and cuddling the fractious child as he walked along the landing. 'Isn't that clever of Mummy?'

'It would have been cleverer of Mummy to have realised she was in labour a little earlier,' Ben growled affectionately from the bottom of the stairs. 'Bring him down. She's respectable for a minute.'

Andy carried Thomas downstairs and into the kitchen, a lump forming in his throat. Daisy was smiling down at the baby in her arms, Ben was looking swamped with emotion and it was getting pretty mutual.

'Anything I can do?'

'Yes. Put Thomas in his high chair and hold the baby while I sort Daisy out.'

He handed him the streaky little bundle, and he sat down at the kitchen table next to Thomas and chatted to them both while Ben took care of his wife.

He could hear Stanley whining softly, and then his phone rang, so he slid it out of his pocket and spoke to Lucy.

'I'm at the Walkers'. Daisy just had the baby. I ran past and she was in the front garden looking out for Ben.'

'What! What is it? Are they all right?'

'A girl, and they're fine. Ben's home now, just in time. I'll stay here for a bit, as long as they need me, and then I'll come home, OK?'

'OK. Are you all right?'

He laughed softly. 'I'm fine. Just fine. I'll see you soon.'

He was fine, he realised. This was what life was about, not going back to work before he was ready. What was that saying? Nobody ever died wishing they'd spent another day at the office?

And anyway, there was still plenty more to do at home.

The feeling of euphoria lasted a whole three days.

Then an envelope arrived from the exam board, dropping innocently to the mat in a clutch of Christmas cards.

'This is for you,' Lucy said, handing it to him at the kitchen table, and he put his mug down and stared at it as if it was poisoned.

'Well, aren't you going to open it?'

'No point,' he said flatly. 'I know what it says.'

'How do you know?'

'Because I screwed up!' he yelled, losing it. He slammed his chair back and it hit the wall, and Lottie started to cry, but he wasn't there to see it. He'd gone, grabbing his coat and disappearing out of the door.

The sound of the slam reverberated around the house, and Lucy picked the baby up and shushed her comfortingly. 'It's all right, darling, Daddy's just struggling a bit,' she said, struggling herself against the tears.

'Da-da,' Lottie said, peering over her shoulder, her bottom lip wobbling.

'He'll be back,' she said reassuringly, but she needed reassurance as much as Lottie, because she wasn't sure when he'd be back, or what mood he'd be in.

She stared at the envelope lying harmlessly on the table where he'd dropped it like a hand grenade.

Should she pull the pin out?

'You passed.'

He stopped in the doorway and stared at her. She was sitting on the stairs, the letter in her hands, and the house was quiet. Lottie must be asleep, he realised, and closed the door quietly.

'So what?' he said. It made no difference. He couldn't use the qualification, and all the course had done was ruin his marriage.

'So what? What do you mean, so what? You really wanted to do this course. You said it was important. If it wasn't important, why the hell did you do it?'

'I have no idea,' he said, and snatching the letter from her, he took it into the study and shut the door firmly.

It was a minute before he could look at it, and then the print blurred. Of all the useless pieces of paper...

He filed it, just because he was like that, and when he came out she was upstairs with Lottie, changing her nappy.

'I'm going in the garden,' he said, and got the shredder and loppers out of the shed and started savaging the hedge that bordered the drive. It was hanging over the gravel, restricting the turning space, and it needed cutting back.

So he cut it.

Hard.

Lucy watched him from the bedroom window, wincing as he decimated the bushes. Hopefully they'd recover, she thought, and she finished putting away the washing and carried Lottie downstairs, putting her on her play mat with a pile of toys while she wrote the last of the Christmas cards.

She made herself a cup of coffee to help the task along, but she just felt sick. She hated it when he was so upset, hated it when she couldn't reach him, but in this mood he was best left alone to work it out for himself.

She pushed the coffee away, finished the cards and put Lottie in the buggy. 'We're going to the post office,' she told him, pausing beside him on the drive.

He didn't stop, just grunted and carried on hacking, and

she winced again and left him to it. There was nothing she could do to help him, and there was something she'd been meaning to do for days.

She went to the post office, bought a card and some flowers and a present for Thomas, and took them round to Daisy.

'Wow, you're looking well,' she said when Daisy opened the door.

'I am. I'm so grateful to Andy, he was amazing, so calm. I was just totally freaked out. He's a good doctor.'

She swallowed. He *was* a good doctor, but would he ever get the chance to practise again?

For the first time ever, a seed of doubt crept into her mind, and she wondered how he'd cope with that. Not well, if the hedge was anything to go by.

'Do you want a cuddle?' Daisy asked, and handed her the baby.

So small. So fine and dainty and tiny, the little fingers clinging instinctively to hers. She felt a huge lump in her throat and swallowed hard.

'She's beautiful. She's very like you.'

'Well, good, because Thomas is the spitting image of Ben and it strikes me I've done all the work so far,' she said with a laugh. 'Fancy a coffee? You can have it with or without caffeine.'

She stared at the baby. 'Can I have tea?' she said, a little thoughtfully. She couldn't be. Surely not? Even though her cycle hadn't returned yet, they'd been careful.

Except once, the day he'd been told he had a tumour, the day they'd gone to London to see David Cardew. And again in the utility room, she remembered. OK, twice, then. But even so…

'Are you all right?' Daisy asked, and she looked up and met her eyes and found a smile.

'I'm fine. Just amazed at how tiny she is. I'd sort of forgotten how small they are.'

'I know. She makes Thomas seem enormous. Biscuit?'

'Thanks.'

It was plain, thankfully, just a simple shortcake biscuit, and she dunked it in her tea and nibbled it and chatted to Daisy while her thoughts whirled round and round.

CHAPTER TEN

THE hedge was trashed.

She'd known it would be, but then he started on the back garden and she couldn't watch it any longer so she tackled him about it.

'Andy, what are you doing?' she asked. 'I know you're angry and frustrated, but you can't just take it out on the garden. There won't be anything left at this rate.'

He straightened up, threw the loppers down on the ground and pushed past her in the doorway.

'Hey, Andy, talk to me.'

'There's nothing to say.'

'There is. Please. Come on. Don't be mad with me.'

'I'm not mad with you. I'm just—'

He stopped, standing there in the kitchen with a closed look on his face, and she put her arms round him and held him. He didn't move, didn't react, didn't return the embrace, and she felt despair swamp her.

She let him go and put the kettle on.

'I've been to see Daisy,' she told him. 'The baby's beautiful.'

'I know. I was there, remember? Their perfect baby in their perfect house in their perfect life—'

'Andy! What the hell's got into you? We've got a pretty good life—'

'Have we? You didn't think so a few weeks ago. You threw me out, remember?'

She felt sick. 'We just needed space.'

'Space? How much space do you need? You told me not to come back.'

'Is that what this is all about? Because you got your work/life balance in a knot?'

'It wasn't in a knot. They were short staffed, they needed cover, and it's my job. I wasn't prepared to let them down by failing in my duty. I've worked damned hard to get where I am, and I've done it all for us. Everything I've done, I've done for us. You know that, but it's not enough. It's never enough. It doesn't matter what I do, it's wrong. I spend too much time at work, too much time away from the family neglecting the house and the garden, and it's wrong. And then I'm here and I do it and it's wrong again.'

'But you're just overdoing it. You're so driven all the time. You say it's for us, but it's not, it's for you, because you're obsessional and you can't seem to see that. Sometimes I think I don't know who you are any more!'

'I just want things to be right,' he said stubbornly. 'That doesn't make me obsessional.'

'It does if your priorities are wrong,' she said gently.

'How is making sure my family is cared for wrong?' he asked, his voice curt.

She sighed and stepped back, searching his eyes. 'It isn't. But it's not everything. We don't just need you working for us like some kind of robot. We need the human side of you, the loving father. And I want the man I married.'

Except he seemed to have disappeared without trace. He still hadn't told her again that he loved her, not since he'd been under the influence of David's 'happy drugs'. Maybe she should ask him for some more of them and slip them into Andy's tea.

Or maybe she should just accept that he didn't love her, after all, was just doing his duty because that was the kind of man he was, and he'd never shirk his duty, not to anyone.

In which case, she just hoped to goodness she wasn't pregnant, because the last thing they needed was yet another child for him to feel dutiful about.

She turned away.

'It's the nativity play tomorrow morning, and Megan's torn her costume so I've got to go over to the school and see if I can fix it,' she said, and putting Lottie in the buggy, she left him to get on with whatever he wanted to do, because right then, she was all out of words on the subject of their marriage.

She didn't even know if she still had one.

He'd massacred the garden.

He stood in it, staring at the mess he'd made and wondering what had possessed him.

Guilt? Grief? Uncertainty?

All of them, probably.

Lucy was right. Ever since his parents had died, he'd been driven, and it was wrecking their lives. And the garden, apparently. He cleared up the prunings, shredding them and scattering the shreddings under the shrubs because there was no room for them in the compost bin, and then he put the tools away and showered and went into town.

He'd had a call from the jewellers to say that the ring was ready, and he needed to collect it.

It looked beautiful. The repair was seamless, the worn side built up so that the diamonds were secure, and it was dazzling.

Would she even want it? She'd told him just a few hours ago that she didn't know who he was. Well, he didn't, either. She wanted the man she'd married, but he wasn't that man any more. That man had been articulate, calm under pressure, good in a crisis, able to handle anything that came into the ED with confidence. Now, he couldn't even recall the names of the drugs.

How could he ask her to bind herself to him for eternity?

He went with Lucy to the nativity play in the morning. The children were desperately excited, and Emily didn't seem to believe that he was coming.

'Will you really be there?' she asked, and he felt the crush of guilt again.

'Yes, Em, I'll really be there. I promise.'

And he was, sitting somewhere in the middle with Lucy, Lottie climbing around on his lap and jumping up and down and grabbing his hair until Lucy took her away because she was tugging on his still-tender scalp.

When the girls came on stage, he could see Emily scanning the crowd looking for them, and she spotted him and beamed. He swallowed. He'd missed all of the plays to date, but so did most of the fathers. It was pretty much unavoidable and there were children whose fathers commuted to London on a daily basis. They were surely never there.

But Ben was there, on paternity leave now, with Thomas and Daisy at his side and the new baby in his arms, watching Florence, and they looked across and smiled. The perfect family? Maybe. Lucky them, he thought bleakly.

James was right. He should enjoy this time with his family, relish every moment of it because he was lucky to have it. So he did. He laughed, he got a lump in his throat when Emily got her words right, and he tried not to laugh when Megan tripped over her costume.

It was an interesting nativity play. The wise men brought peace, harmony and co-operation, the stable was a garden shed and Mary and Joseph were on their way to visit their family, the Christmas story with a twist.

Peace, harmony and co-operation, he thought. If only. Lucy had hardly spoken to him since yesterday, and she looked peaky and troubled. He thought of the ring, stashed safely in a locked drawer in his desk. Would she accept it?

He had no idea.

'Did you like me? I got my words right!' Emily said, bouncing with excitement as they walked home laden with shoe-bags and PE kit and paintings.

'You did. Well done.'

'And did you see me? I nearly felled off the stage!' Megan told him.

'But you didn't, and you were very good. You were both good.'

'Florence wanted to have Henrietta as baby Jesus, but Daisy wouldn't let her. She said she was too small and she might cry, so we had Jasmine's doll. It wees.'

'Does it?' he said, trying not to laugh.

'Only if you give it water,' Emily said. 'Miss Richards said we couldn't give it water so it wouldn't wee on the stage.'

'Good idea,' he said, glancing at Lucy, but her smile was strained and she didn't look at him, and his heart sank.

So much for peace and harmony…

'Can we put the tree up, Mummy? Please, please!'

Megan was fizzing with excitement, but Lucy felt hollow inside. Only not so hollow.

'I expect so, if your father can get it out of the loft.'

'Can we have a real one?' Emily asked, tugging at him. 'They smell so lovely.'

'Can we?' he asked Lucy, knowing she'd have an opinion.

'We can't all fit in the car with a tree.'

'I'll go, then,' he said, and then remembered. 'Or I'll look after the children, rather, and you can go.'

'They've got them at the garden centre round the corner. It's only a few hundred yards. Can you carry it that far?'

'I expect so, if it's not eight foot tall.'

'Right. Well, you take the girls and I'll stay here with Lottie and find the decorations,' she said, so they put their coats on and headed off.

The girls all but dragged him to the little garden centre, and as soon as they arrived he knew he was in trouble.

'Daddy, look! They've got Santa's Grotto! Please can we go and see him? Please please please please *pleeeeeease*!'

He looked down at Emily, her little face beseeching, and then Megan, eyes like saucers, bouncing next to him and joining in the begging, and he crumpled.

'I'll call Mummy,' he said, and pulled his phone out. 'Luce, hi. We may be a while. They've got Santa.'

'Oh, the girls'll love it!'

She sounded wistful, as if she'd like to be there. And why not?

'Why don't you come?' he urged, suddenly needing to have all of them together for this. 'Bring Lottie down. It's her first Christmas and she's never seen him. We'll wait for you.'

'OK,' she said, and he grinned at the girls.

'Mummy's coming and bringing Lottie to see him, too,' he told them, and their little faces lit up.

'Yay! We can see him! We can see Santa!' Emily squealed, bouncing on the spot.

'I tell you what, shall we go and choose a tree while we wait, and they can keep it for us till we go?' he suggested, hoping the distraction would help to keep a lid on their excitement until Lucy got there.

It worked, to his relief. They found the trees, all lined up against the fence, and started to look through them, discussing their flaws and failings. They were a motley collection, because it was only two days to Christmas and they'd left it a bit late to choose a real one, but it was what Emily wanted, and he wanted to give her what she wanted this year, because last year he hadn't even been here for most of it.

He chose the bushiest one which seemed well balanced, and they paid for it and had it put on one side. By the time they'd done that, Lucy had arrived with Lottie, to his relief, so with the girls fizzing with excitement again they went and queued outside Santa's Grotto.

It was pretty makeshift, but the girls didn't seem to mind, and after a mercifully short time they reached the front of the queue and went in together as a family.

'Three beautiful little girls? Ho-ho-ho,' the jolly Santa said, beaming. 'Come and sit here and tell me your name,' he said to Emily, and she perched on the stool beside him and told him her name.

'And what do you want for Christmas, Emily?' he asked cheerfully.

'I want my Daddy to be better,' she said, her eyes welling, and Andy felt as if he'd been hit in the chest.

He sucked in a breath and met the startled man's eyes.

'Has your Daddy been ill?'

She nodded. 'He had something nasty growing in his head and it was pressing on his brain, but they cut it out and now he's getting better, but it's too slow and it makes him cross and he makes Mummy cry.'

Oh, God. Why, *why* had he thought this was a good idea?

'I'm OK,' he said, his voice ragged with emotion. 'Em, I'm OK, darling. I'm getting better.'

'Really? Promise?'

'Really. Really and truly, I promise. I'm just bad tempered because it's taking a long time, and I'm sorry. I don't mean to be...'

He felt Lucy squeeze his arm, and he sucked in another breath and tried to crush down the emotion that was overwhelming him.

'I'm sure you don't,' their Santa said softly. 'Well, young lady, I'll have a word with the elves and we'll see what we can do, but I think if you were to give your Daddy a cuddle, it would be all the Christmas present he would need, and I'm sure it would make him feel much better.'

She nodded, sniffing, and he leant forwards and patted her hand. 'Is there anything else you'd like?'

She shook her head. 'Not really. Just my Daddy back.'

'Well, why don't you go and give him that cuddle and see if it works?' he suggested gently.

She ran to him, burying her face in his coat, and he hugged her close, lifting her into his arms and cuddling her tight. He left Lucy dealing with Megan and Lottie. He had no idea what Megan asked for, or what Lottie made of the strange man with the crazy beard and the funny costume. He just held Emily tight until she stopped clinging to him, and then he kissed her gently and put her down, and they walked out together, Em's hand firmly in his.

'Are you OK?' Lucy asked quietly, and he could see that her lashes were clogged with tears.

'Just about,' he said gruffly. 'Luce, I'm sorry. I didn't know I made you cry.'

'Shh,' she murmured, her voice gentle. 'It's OK, Andy. It's just been a bit tough for all of us, but we're getting there.' They walked through the shop part, and she suddenly stopped and clapped her hands together. 'Hey, girls, why don't we go and choose some more decorations for the tree?'

Bless her for distracting them. They found a 'Baby's First Christmas' bauble for Lottie, and a little red stocking to hang on the fireplace with the others, and a new angel for the top of the tree. And then they collected the tree and he carried it home.

By the time they got there he was regretting not going for a scrawny one, but once it was in the pot and his arm had stopped aching, he was sure it would be fine.

'It's a bit crooked, Daddy,' Em said, snuggling up to him and studying it thoughtfully.

It was. The trunk kinked half way up and then carried on straight up, so if they looked at it side on they could see it, but it went in a corner so it didn't really matter. And Emily was right, it did smell lovely.

'Daddy, Daddy, you have to do the lights,' Megan said, dragging them out of the box.

'Carefully. Give them to me.'

He untangled them, which would have been easier without his helper, and threaded them round the tree, and then the girls and Lucy hung the baubles on it, Em and Megan doing the lowest ones, Lucy standing on a chair while he held it steady so she could do the higher ones.

She leant over to put the new angel on the top and he put his hands on her hips and anchored her, then lifted her down and kissed her. Just a fleeting touch of his lips, but she seemed a little distracted and he didn't know why.

'That looks lovely,' she said, smiling brightly, but he could see it didn't quite reach her eyes. 'Good work, everyone. Shall we have some tea and cake?'

'Yay, cake!' Em said, dancing into the kitchen on tiptoes, and he cleared up the boxes and put them back in the loft, wondering what was wrong with Lucy.

Was she getting round to telling him that this would be their last Christmas together as a family? He didn't know, and he'd given up trying to second-guess her, but then he hadn't realised that he'd made her cry, either.

Feeling slightly sick with apprehension, he went back down to the kitchen.

'Don't give me any cake,' he told her. 'I've got things to do.'

And he shut himself in his study, sat down at his desk and unlocked the drawer. The ring, nestled in its original velvet box, sparkled at him mockingly.

'Oh, Lucy,' he sighed, and shut the drawer, locked it again and took Stanley for a walk.

The supermarket would be a nightmare, and going there was the last thing she wanted to do after she finished her surgery on Christmas Eve morning. She hadn't wanted to work the shift, and she remembered the grief she'd given Andy just a year ago because he'd been working Christmas Eve.

She felt such a hypocrite, and racked with guilt, because she realised now that sometimes you just had to do what you had to do, no matter how unwelcome it might be.

Like the last-minute shopping. She'd done most of the shopping a few days earlier, but there were a few things she still had to get, so she dived into the supermarket on the way home and got the rest.

Not that she felt like cooking. The queasiness she'd been feeling for the last week or so was still there, lurking in the background, and just to set her mind at rest she picked up a pregnancy test on her way to the checkout.

It burned a hole in her handbag all the way home, and

she unloaded the shopping, opened the fridge and saw the turkey and the stuffing, and drew the line.

She'd do it tomorrow morning. No doubt the children would be up at six at the latest, so there'd be plenty of time to stuff it and get it in the oven in time. They were watching a film on the television, Andy in the middle, Lottie asleep on his lap and the girls on either side snuggled up against him.

Taking the slim box out of her handbag, she went upstairs to their bathroom, locked the door and opened the packet.

'Is that everything?'

'I think so,' he said. 'I hope so. There seems to be a lot.'

The girls were finally in bed asleep, and they were on the floor by the tree, stacking presents for the children.

'They're all for the children,' she told him, feeling flat and despondent and tearful. 'I haven't got you a present. I didn't know what to get you. It's not that I didn't want to give you anything, I just feel I don't know you any more, and I had no idea what you'd like.'

His eyes softened. 'Oh, Lucy, you don't need to give me anything.'

'There is one thing,' she said, her heart hitching a little. 'It's not really a present, and I don't know if you'll even want it, but it's a bit late to worry about that now. It's not the sort of thing you can take back.' She took a deep breath, then said, 'I'm pregnant.'

'Preg—? Oh, Lucy.' He gathered her into his arms, cradling her against his chest and feeling the joy burst in his heart. 'Oh, that's amazing,' he said, not knowing whether to laugh or cry. 'How could you think I wouldn't want another baby?'

'Because you didn't want Lottie?'

He was stunned. 'Of course I wanted her! I love her to bits.'

'But you were never here for her, you hardly paid any attention to her when you were here, and I thought you didn't want her, didn't love her. Didn't love any of us any more.'

'Of course I love you. I love all of you—Lucy, how could you think that?'

'Because you never *tell* us. The only time in ages you've told me that you love me, you were under the influence of David's "happy drugs".'

He swallowed hard, remembering the burning, desperate need to say those words to her. 'I thought it might be my last chance, that if I lost my speech permanently, I'd never be able to say it again. I didn't know if you'd want to hear it, but I wanted you to know. Just for the record. And I know I've been difficult. I know I'm not easy to live with, I know I drive myself too hard, I know I try and overcompensate because of my parents, go too far the other way, but it doesn't mean I don't love you. I do love you. I love you so much it's hard to find the words, even under normal circumstances.'

'Well, you seem to be doing all right at the moment,' she said tearfully.

He gave a hollow laugh and shook his head, then stood up and lifted a tiny little parcel from the tree.

'This is for you. I don't know if you'll want it, or if it's the last thing in the world you want from me, but it's how I feel about you, and I should have shown you years ago. But I don't want you feeling pressured by it. I love you. I want to make our marriage work, I always have, and I'm not very good at it, but I'm willing to try, and the last thing I'm going to do is walk away from you, ever. But if you want to walk away from me, if that's what's right for you, then I'll understand, because I'm not the man you married. I don't know what's going to happen about my speech, I still have problems, and I may never be able to go back to my job again, and that changes things, I know that, so I can't ask you to stay if you feel it's wrong for you.'

She stared at him, then down at the tiny parcel he'd put in her hands. There was a fine gold ribbon round it, and she pulled the bow and it fell away. The paper was meticulously folded round it, perfectly creased, and she unwrapped it and a small velvet box fell into her hand.

It had a tiny gold clasp on one side, and hinges on the other, and it looked very old. A ring box?

She lifted the catch and opened the lid, and gasped.

'Andy!' she breathed, and then her eyes flooded with tears. 'Oh, Andy, it's beautiful.'

'It's an eternity ring,' he said gruffly, 'because that's how long I'll love you.'

Tears cascaded down her cheeks, and she lifted the ring out of the box and gave it to him, her fingers shaking.

'Put it on my finger, please?' she asked him softly, and with hands that shook slightly, he slid it on. It settled there next to her other two rings as if it had been made for it, and she stared down at them and sniffed.

'Oh, Andy, it's perfect. Where did you find it?'

'In the jewellers' in town. It had only just come in the day before, and it had to be cleaned and repaired, because it was a little worn on one side, but it just seemed to have your name written all over it, and it was the right size.'

'How did you know?'

'I took your engagement ring with me.'

'The day I couldn't find it,' she said, realising what he'd done.

He nodded.

'I can't believe you thought I didn't love you any more,' she said.

'You haven't told me recently, either,' he pointed out. 'I've been too busy making sure all the boxes were ticked, and you've just been left to muddle along in the chaos that I've left behind.'

She nodded.

'We've been pretty rubbish, haven't we?' she agreed.

'We have. Shall we start again?'

'Good idea. I love you. And it doesn't matter to me if you go back to work or not, you're still the man I love and you always will be. I just might have to hide the garden tools.'

He laughed softly, then his smile grew tender. 'I love you, too. And I'm sorry you had to throw me out to get me to come to my senses. Thank you for standing by me through all of this. It would have been so easy to walk away, especially the way I've been.'

'It would never be easy to walk away from you,' she said, remembering the day he'd gone. 'I thought my heart would break when I heard that door close behind you. And when I realised you were so ill, when I thought I might lose you for ever—'

He scooped her up in his arms and settled down with her on the sofa, cradled on his lap. 'You haven't lost me. You'll never really lose me, whatever happens. I'll always love you.'

'I hope so. I'm banking on it.' She went quiet for a moment, then tilted her head so she could see his eyes. 'What was in the letter?'

He went very still, then gave a wry smile. 'Ah. A lot of soul-baring. I'm surprised you didn't read it.'

'I didn't want to. I thought—I'd rather you told me yourself.'

He nodded. 'I've still got it. It's in my desk.'

'Can I read it?'

He hesitated briefly, then nodded again. 'Sure. I'll get it.'

He shifted her off his lap, brought it to her and then sat down quietly at the other end of the sofa.

Fingers trembling slightly, she peeled up the flap of the envelope and pulled out the single sheet. The writing was untidy, the ink smudged in places.

Tears?

She flattened it out with her hand and started to read.

My dearest, darling Lucy

If you're reading this, it's because it's all gone horribly wrong. I hope you never have to. As I write, I'm filled with dread for what the future holds for us all. Not for me. I'm not afraid for me, but for you and the children, because I know the impact of losing your parents is devastating, and I can't bear to think of the children growing up with that sadness hanging over them. I know you'll be amazing with them, loving and supportive, and I hope in time you'll find someone to support you, too, hopefully someone who won't let you down as I have.

This is the hardest thing I've ever had to write, and I don't know where to start, except to say I'm sorry that I've somehow hurt you or let you down. I never meant to. Everything I've done, I've done for you, for the family, but that doesn't seem to have been what you wanted. It's too late now to change, too late to do anything about it except to apologise with all my heart for failing you, for letting our marriage get brushed aside by other things.

You have been my reason for living, the only thing that's got me through the tough times, the best thing that's ever happened to me. The ten years I've been privileged to be with you have been the happiest and most fulfilling of my life, and I'm gutted at the thought that all of that might be gone, wiped away by this crazy thing in my head.

Even if I live, I might be unable to function normally, might be unable to communicate or understand, paralysed—who knows? And I cannot bear the thought of you tied to me under those conditions. If that is what's happened, then please, PLEASE, don't stay with me. I want you to be free, to find a new life with the children, a life of peace. I don't want you staying with me out of guilt or pity, trapped in an impossible situation because of a vow you made to a different man, the man I used to be. I love you far too much to bear that.

Be happy, my darling. Be free of guilt and pain and fear. Love our children for me, and when they ask about me, try and remember the good times.
All my love,
Andy

She felt the tears sliding down her face. One dripped onto the letter, making another smudge to join the others his tears had caused.

She couldn't speak. There was nothing she could say. Maybe nothing *to* say, nothing that mattered any more.

She stood up and walked over to him, curled up on his lap and let him hold her as she cried away the grief and pain and fear that she'd held trapped inside her for months. And then she lifted her head, and kissed away his tears.

One year later...

'Mummy, Mummy, Daddy's home!' Emily shrieked.

Lucy came out of the kitchen wiping her hands on a

tea towel, and kissed him. 'Hi,' she said, her eyes smiling. 'How was work?'

How was it? Great, was how it was. Great that he was back, great that, after a month of supervision, he'd been passed as fit to work alone since May. He'd done what James had suggested, taken his time, waited until he was sure he was all right rather than rush it and go back too soon, and he'd spent that extra time with his family.

And as a result of that experience, he'd only gone back part time, job sharing with a woman who had a young family, and it was panning out really well. He had time for the children, time for Lucy and time for himself. It was a win-win situation, and he loved it.

'Work was fine. Good. Surprisingly quiet, thankfully. How are you? Are you coping with all the Christmas chaos?'

She chuckled. 'I'm fine. I'm glad you're home promptly, though.'

'I promised I would be,' he said pointedly, and she smiled, because these days, if he promised something, he did it. No messing. No ifs or buts, nothing getting in the way, because he'd learned that he wasn't indispensable to anyone but his family, and they always came first, without exception.

'It's so nice to be home with you,' he said softly. 'I didn't know what I was missing before.'

She smiled and kissed him again, lingering this time a moment longer. 'Mum and Dad have arrived. Go and say hello and then come and open a bottle. You're off now for three days, and I intend to make sure you relax.'

'You do that,' he said, grinning, and he went into the sitting room and scooped Daniel off the floor. 'Hello, monster, how are you?' he asked, tucking the giggling baby into the crook of his arm and greeting his in-laws warmly.

'I think Lucy's got some champagne in the fridge. Can I tempt you?'

'I think that would be lovely,' Lucy's mother said, getting to her feet and kissing his cheek.

They followed him into the kitchen, and he stole a slice of bread with smoked salmon on it. 'Yum. Hi, Lottie. Hi, Megan.'

'Hi, Daddy,' they chorused, and he handed Daniel over to his grandfather and popped the cork on the champagne, then raised his glass.

'Happy families,' he said, and the adults echoed him.

'It's not happy families, silly, it's Happy Christmas!' Megan told him, laughing, but he just grinned at her and hugged her.

'Same thing, isn't it?' he said, and over the top of her glass Lucy smiled at him, her eyes filled with love and laughter.

'Definitely. I couldn't have put it better myself…'

* * * * *

Mills & Boon® Hardback

December 2012

ROMANCE

A Ring to Secure His Heir	Lynne Graham
What His Money Can't Hide	Maggie Cox
Woman in a Sheikh's World	Sarah Morgan
At Dante's Service	Chantelle Shaw
At His Majesty's Request	Maisey Yates
Breaking the Greek's Rules	Anne McAllister
The Ruthless Caleb Wilde	Sandra Marton
The Price of Success	Maya Blake
The Man From her Wayward Past	Susan Stephens
Blame it on the Bikini	Natalie Anderson
The English Lord's Secret Son	Margaret Way
The Secret That Changed Everything	Lucy Gordon
Baby Under the Christmas Tree	Teresa Carpenter
The Cattleman's Special Delivery	Barbara Hannay
Secrets of the Rich & Famous	Charlotte Phillips
Her Man In Manhattan	Trish Wylie
His Bride in Paradise	Joanna Neil
Christmas Where She Belongs	Meredith Webber

MEDICAL

From Christmas to Eternity	Caroline Anderson
Her Little Spanish Secret	Laura Iding
Christmas with Dr Delicious	Sue MacKay
One Night That Changed Everything	Tina Beckett

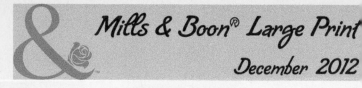

Mills & Boon® Large Print

December 2012

ROMANCE

Contract with Consequences	Miranda Lee
The Sheikh's Last Gamble	Trish Morey
The Man She Shouldn't Crave	Lucy Ellis
The Girl He'd Overlooked	Cathy Williams
Mr Right, Next Door!	Barbara Wallace
The Cowboy Comes Home	Patricia Thayer
The Rancher's Housekeeper	Rebecca Winters
Her Outback Rescuer	Marion Lennox
A Tainted Beauty	Sharon Kendrick
One Night With The Enemy	Abby Green
The Dangerous Jacob Wilde	Sandra Marton

HISTORICAL

A Not So Respectable Gentleman?	Diane Gaston
Outrageous Confessions of Lady Deborah	Marguerite Kaye
His Unsuitable Viscountess	Michelle Styles
Lady with the Devil's Scar	Sophia James
Betrothed to the Barbarian	Carol Townend

MEDICAL

Sydney Harbour Hospital: Bella's Wishlist	Emily Forbes
Doctor's Mile-High Fling	Tina Beckett
Hers For One Night Only?	Carol Marinelli
Unlocking the Surgeon's Heart	Jessica Matthews
Marriage Miracle in Swallowbrook	Abigail Gordon
Celebrity in Braxton Falls	Judy Campbell

Mills & Boon® Hardback

January 2013

ROMANCE

MEDICAL

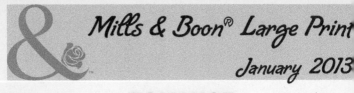
Mills & Boon® *Large Print*

January 2013

ROMANCE

Unlocking her Innocence	Lynne Graham
Santiago's Command	Kim Lawrence
His Reputation Precedes Him	Carole Mortimer
The Price of Retribution	Sara Craven
The Valtieri Baby	Caroline Anderson
Slow Dance with the Sheriff	Nikki Logan
Bella's Impossible Boss	Michelle Douglas
The Tycoon's Secret Daughter	Susan Meier
Just One Last Night	Helen Brooks
The Greek's Acquisition	Chantelle Shaw
The Husband She Never Knew	Kate Hewitt

HISTORICAL

His Mask of Retribution	Margaret McPhee
How to Disgrace a Lady	Bronwyn Scott
The Captain's Courtesan	Lucy Ashford
Man Behind the Façade	June Francis
The Highlander's Stolen Touch	Terri Brisbin

MEDICAL

Sydney Harbour Hospital: Marco's Temptation	Fiona McArthur
Waking Up With His Runaway Bride	Louisa George
The Legendary Playboy Surgeon	Alison Roberts
Falling for Her Impossible Boss	Alison Roberts
Letting Go With Dr Rodriguez	Fiona Lowe
Dr Tall, Dark...and Dangerous?	Lynne Marshall